About

Larry G. Goldsmith is a financial forensic sleuth. He is a career licensed Illinois attorney, certified public accountant and financial forensic accountant. Being a financial detective led him to pursue writing fiction in his off-hour. Historical fiction is his passion as he revisits times forgotten while telling a romantic tale.

He brings a passion and skill to his story-telling weaving his legal and sleuth skills into the story. Like the author his protagonists are moral and ethical individuals who are not perfect and acknowledge their mistakes. The reader will find the characters as everyday people that they know and like.

Larry is a member of various professional legal and accounting organizations and has testified as an expert witness in both federal and state courts. His hobbies include bicycling, writing, exploring other cultures and, when younger, whitewater kayaking and volleyball.

MARC MARCI

LARRY G. GOLDSMITH

MARC MARCI

Vanguard Press

VANGUARD PAPERBACK

A CIP catalogue record for this title is
available from the British Library.

ISBN 978 1 784659 94 3

*Vanguard Press is an imprint of
Pegasus Elliot MacKenzie Publishers Ltd.*
www.pegasuspublishers.com

First Published in 2021

**Vanguard Press
Sheraton House Castle Park
Cambridge England**

Printed & Bound in Great Britain

Dedication

To those who have struggled and are struggling to discover their inner self – this is for you.

Acknowledgements

Thank you to my friends and family who have supported and encouraged me as I have pursued my passion. Without you, my first novel would have been an unfulfilled dream.

Acknowledgements

Prologue

We all have secrets. Some days, we fear others will discover our past indiscretions. Other days, we forget that we had a past, and live under the illusion that time erased our sins. That's how it was for me. Today, I have no memory of the boy I'd been. This morning, I wasn't mediating on my past, rather I was thinking of the things I needed to do.

I was tempted to stay in bed awhile, but my children needed me. In a few minutes, the kids would need to be dressed and taken to daycare. I walked to the end of the driveway, grabbed the newspaper, and returned to the kitchen. I glanced at the front page as I toasted the multigrain bread and made breakfast. I took out my home-made strawberry preserves and poured two cups of milk: one in a sippy and the other in a cup with fish decorations.

Barefoot in my bathrobe, I scanned the newspaper knowing these were my last few minutes of solitude before the kids would come thumping down the stairs. I should have been cutting up fruit for their yogurt breakfast, but instead I read the newspaper, savoring the peaceful silence in the house while they were still asleep.

A headline grabbed my attention.

Escapee arrested after thirty-five years on the run.

The article said a fugitive had been arrested and convicted of robbing a bank when he was barely eighteen. Shortly after his conviction, he escaped from jail. He hid out in a small rural town, working under an assumed identity, for the town's car mechanic. The old mechanic had a son who died as a child and saw this troubled soul as his son's replacement. So, the escapee lived a life under the deceased child's identity and social security number. The mechanic became the young man's father figure that he never had. In time, the convict bought the shop and expanded the operations to sell car and truck parts.

Over the years the convict settled down, married, and had children and grandchildren. It wasn't until his grandson applied to the Naval Academy and the government conducted its routine security check, that the man's identity was discovered. Over three decades after the original conviction, a cold case detective showed up with an arrest warrant. The town's most respected citizen had a criminal past. But was he truly still a criminal? Or had years of a life rehabilitated absolved him of his illegal past? Lost in thought, I ignored my parental responsibilities.

Suddenly, I looked at the clock. "Oh no! Kids, it's time to wake up. We need to get going."

I rushed the children through breakfast, and I was able to drop Georgia off at preschool on time. On the drive home, I switched off the *Frozen* soundtrack and listened to the radio instead. The DJ's first song brought back memories of a time; a lifetime ago. The song reminded me of my youth, before I became who I am today. I thought of the convict and his grandchildren in that small town. Like him, I had a secret life that has remained hidden under layers of years.

It was one of those gorgeous, sunny Ohio days; the beginning of Indian summer. Few leaves had fallen to the ground and the trees resembled a beautiful Monet painting, changing from green to mesmerizing shades of orange, bright-red, auburn-red, and brown. The nights were cool, but comfortable. Days like this always brought me back to my adolescence when I lived with my folks in the house on Maple Street. Dragon's breath and wild delphinium bloomed in my neighbors' gardens then, too. I had my whole life ahead of me and, like a flower, all I had to do was soak up the sun.

Life was so simple in those days. I could not have foreseen how quickly it could get complicated, or how my entanglements would shape my destiny.

Chapter 1

Imagine a brown-haired, scrawny, five-foot-six-inch kid preparing to enter college in a few months. I had been accepted into Northwestern University McCormick School of Engineering, one of the top five schools in the country for software engineering majors. Mom bragged to anyone who would listen that her only child was brilliant. I was scheduled to graduate high school early, in January.

I grabbed a Pop Tart and a Gatorade and started out the door to band practice. I heard my mother call for me. "Marc?"

I stopped in my tracks, "Yes, Mom?"

"Did you fill out the housing forms for college? You know they are due."

My mom was even more excited about my admission to Northwestern than I was. She'd posted a picture of my acceptance letter on her Facebook page. My dad emailed all his friends the news about my early admission. He had a photocopy of the 'yes' on his office door.

I'd spent my whole life getting ready for college.

The truth was, my friends and I were nerds. I had a lonely existence since most of my friends I had met online, and didn't know their real names; only their monikers. For enjoyment, I read programming manuals and conquered computer games the way other kids took apart candy wrappers. I spent hours calculating the path to a game's highest levels. I hoped Northwestern would provide me with friends and a social life.

"Yes, Mom. And I signed up for my classes and I'll download my textbooks once I receive a confirmation that I have the classes and know the assigned reading materials. It's only September! We have plenty of time before the deadline."

She blew a kiss in my direction as I once again walked out of the rear door. I wasn't expecting to see my parents again until Monday because this was their long romantic weekend together. They wanted to witness the changing autumn leaves on the roads less traveled, away from the city noise. As I strolled down the driveway, I saw their bicycles had been loaded onto the roof of the SUV. Their favorite spot was near Kent, Ohio, where the countryside offered miles of open road and stunning views.

My parents were lovers and best friends. Then, I prayed I would find a spouse who would affectionately love me. They frequently walked in the park or rode their bicycles on excursions across the neighborhood's bike trails. Some afternoons, they simply sat on the shores of Lake Erie listening to the waves and experiencing the sunset with a bottle of chilled white wine and cheese.

When Mom and Dad were away, I didn't mind spending the entire weekend alone with my computers and games. This next couple of days I planned to best a new game, so I was grateful that there would be no one to tell me to go outside and get fresh air. Besides, the refrigerator was stocked and there was no one to tell me not to eat in my bedroom.

Band practice was twice a week. The school band leader marched us up and down the football field, rehearsing in preparation for Friday night's last football game of the season. In Ohio, football was holy. It was more than a sport.

Heaven forbid, any of us made a mistake, like playing a wrong note or tune. The leader would yell, "The half-time performance must be *perfect*. We need to practice until it is without errors."

That Friday afternoon, we were performing at the school's indoor pep rally in the gymnasium. We blasted our instruments as the football players' names were announced to the school body. The cheerleaders ran out to get the audience amped. Their routine was my favorite part of the school pep rallies. I couldn't tear my eyes away from their tiny, short skirts and halter tops, or the way their uniforms revealed flat, muscular midriffs and legs.

Lisa was the squad's captain. She initiated the group's routine by tumbling through the air and landing on the ground with her legs split apart and her pom-poms raised high above her head. I couldn't stop staring at Lisa; she was a hot blonde and *the* most popular girl at the school. Like most of the beautiful people, she didn't know I was alive. Lisa was prom queen, president of the Student Council and had been accepted to the Liberal Arts College at Penn State. She was perfect.

I was jealous of her popularity and, secretly, I wished I could *be* her. She was drop dead gorgeous and publicly she was a friendly person. I was frustrated as the only remaining virgin in the senior class who was never invited to the senior year parties.

I adjusted my stupid white band hat as Lisa and the other cheerleaders did cartwheels off the gymnasium floor. As I did so, out of the corner of my eye, I noticed a police officer making his way toward the north end of the stands. He spoke to several people and the students pointed in the band's direction. As he got closer, I slid down in my seat.

"What did you do, Marc?" Jason asked.

Before I could react, the officer was right in front of me. I racked my brain and prayed the games I illegally downloaded were not the reason for this policeman's attention.

"Marc Fields?" the cop said.

I nodded.

"I need you to come with me."

I stood awkwardly and carried my French horn down the bleachers with the policeman trailing behind me. I heard other students whispering my name as they watched me leave the gym.

The officer led me out of the school and then through the chain-link gate that separated the building from the parking lot. His squad car was pulled up right next to the fence, in a no-parking zone. As I walked, I had remorse, but still didn't know what I had done.

I told the police officer, "I need to put my French horn back in its case and put it my car."

The officer responded, "We don't have a lot of time to waste, someone is waiting for us at your home."

"If you have your car here in the lot, then I'll follow you to your home."

I was relieved not to be riding in the back seat of the cruiser, but something about the cop's attitude told me to stay on my guard. He was tense and edgy. He watched me load the French horn into the back seat, wrap my band jacket around it, and buckle the seat belt across it so it wouldn't slide around. I took off my plumed hat and set it in the passenger seat.

While the cop was getting into his car, I quickly texted my Dad. There was no immediate response. I was on my own. Waiting for me in front of my home was another police cruiser. A female police officer got out and deliberately walked toward my car, now parked in front of the garage. I slowly exited the vehicle, not sure if she was going to taser me or what. I had a nervous smile on my face as I greeted her. I prepared my defense while driving home to plead innocent of illegally downloading games and music.

I opened the back door of my car and said loudly, "I'm just getting my French horn."

I blanched when I thought of anyone looking through my browser history. My dad's a lawyer, I thought, he'll know how to defend me when he gets home. I hoisted my French horn on my shoulder as she drew closer to me.

The woman introduced herself. "Marc. My name is Lieutenant Rachel Watson. Please call me Rachel. My partner radioed ahead and told me to come here and meet with you." I was baffled, she was talking like a friend and not an arresting officer. Her words had a note of kind sincerity.

She then asked, "Marc, do you have any brothers, sisters, uncles or aunts?"

"There is my Uncle Jack, uh, Jack Levin. He is my dad's law partner and best friend. He isn't a blood relative. Officer, what's going on? What did I do? Can't you just call my parents? I'll give you their cell number." I couldn't keep the fear out of my voice.

As we walked up the driveway to the house, the policewoman asked, in a compassionate tone, "Marc, let's go into the house and speak. Do you have your uncle's telephone number handy? I will also need to speak with him."

I walked into the kitchen and grabbed Mom's phone book from the junk drawer. I handed it to Lieutenant Watson, who took it and unclipped her cell phone from her belt.

She gave me permission to take my instrument into my bedroom, where I laid the French horn on my bed while hoping that Dad would call me. The police officer had her eye on me as I walked up the stairs which made me nervous.

As I descended the stairs she asked, "Why don't you sit down? I'm going to step outside for a moment to make a phone call. I'll return in a minute."

She stood close enough to the front screen door for me to hear her say my uncle's name into the phone. The house was quiet except for Dad's cuckoo clock, which was whirring in the corner, and the clicking sound the refrigerator made when it went through its cooling cycle.

After what felt like an eternity, Officer Watson opened the door. She smiled at me and sat in my Dad's reading chair, close enough to reach for my hand as I was on the adjacent couch.

"Marc, I've contacted your uncle, and he's on his way. Brace yourself. I need to share some horrific news. Unfortunately, about two hours ago, we received a call from a hospital in Portage, Ohio. Your mother and father were killed while riding their bicycles on a dirt road when a semi-truck passed a slower moving vehicle. The driver did not see your parents."

I was speechless. It was too surreal for me to believe that they would not be returning home on Sunday night. Mom had steaks defrosting in the fridge for Monday. Who was going to cook them now?

My mind and heart said, *"I'll never hear Mom's voice again, or yell at a Cleveland Indians game with my dad."* The silence was deafening. Besides my dad's partner, Jack, I had no one. I was utterly and completely alone in the world with no means of financial support.

Chapter 2

After the initial shock, my mind and memory became a blur. I recall the screen door slamming behind Officer Watson as she saw my uncle's car pull up next to mine. I couldn't hear their words as they talked.

As I helplessly laid in my bed for two days, Jack handled all the funeral arrangements. I remember the funeral home's brown walls and rows of brown chairs. Nameless, faceless people hugged me. The people paying their last respects offered me words of sympathy. But I could not hear or decipher their words through the depressed haze that surrounded me.

I recall when someone took a razor and cut my shirt. Even this ritual didn't faze me. I floated through it. My chest ached with loss and my tears flowed. Jack invited me to his place to stay in the guest room, so I wouldn't be alone. Even though I was eighteen, I felt as weak as a toddler. Jack wrapped his arms around me and held me tight.

At the grave site, each mourner quietly shoveled three mounds of dirt on the two caskets laying side by side in the ground. The sound of the earth as it landed on the plain wooden coffins hit me like a sledgehammer; my parents would never be coming home.

In the hearse, Jack said, "Your father, as you know, was my best friend. I promised him that I would always be here for you. Consider yourself part of our family now and forever."

For the next seven days, I moved back into my parents' home with an excused absence from school. The days passed, but time seemed to stand still. People brought meals to the house; so much food that the fridge was packed with glass pans and plastic containers. Endless numbers of people arrived every night to attend the short religious service and comfort me. Yet, when they went away after seven days, it was just me, Jack and Jack's family. The last thing I wanted to do was eat food made by strangers or sleep down the hallway from my parents' empty bedroom. Nor, did I want to sleep at Jack's home in the den.

The high school guidance counselor, Mrs. O'Hara, called to pay her respects. She cleared it with my teachers to give me a passing grade on missing assignments allowing me to still graduate in January. I thanked her.

Jack looked in on me every day to make sure I was eating and functioning. He heated up one of the meals from the fridge at night for me and kept me company before returning to his home. He pleaded with me to move to his place permanently and be one of his kids. He tried to keep my spirits up. After a week, Jack figuratively kicked me in the butt, forcing me to stay grounded in reality. He reminded me I needed to return to school and my studies if I hoped to graduate.

Sometimes, I caught myself standing in the driveway, looking up the street, as though I was waiting for my parents to appear. I dreamed that I heard my mother making breakfast, or my dad laughing in the living room. I felt their presence in the house.

Daily, Jack assured me that he would be there for me, day or night. He called me every day. I knew he was my friend for life: a mentor, and a second father that I so desperately needed.

Chapter 3

As I walked down the school halls, I could feel the eyes of everyone on me. I could hear my name in the muffled conversations. The teachers turned their faces away as I approached and pretended not to see me. Nobody knew what to say to me, so they ignored me.

Like a robot, I attended each class and returned home each afternoon to my empty abode. Jack thought having a routine would help me get through the grief. The school counselor tried to give me grief therapy, but I didn't have anything to say and her words fell on deaf ears. I told her, "I'm fine. I'm over the mourning and ready to start college soon."

During those months, I gamed more than I ever had before. My weekends were marathon sessions, epic campaigns that ate up my hours. Being online was the only time I didn't feel alone. I had my Internet friends. I didn't have to tell them about the funeral, I could be whoever I wanted to be. We competed to kill a lot of dragons together.

Sometimes, one of my parents' friends called, but we didn't have much to say to each other. They asked me about school, and I told them everything was okay. They wanted to help in some way, but what was the point? It wouldn't bring my parents back. My parents had so many friends keeping their memory alive, but in a way, that was even more painful.

The first frost came, and I could feel the last days of fall's sunshine slipping away. I dreamed about my parents less. Now, when I slept, all I saw was blackness. I woke up in the middle of the night in my parents' king-sized bed, hugging Mom's pillow, as if it was her body. I was going crazy without them: it was time to make a change.

In mid-December, winter break arrived. Jack called and said that he was coming over to take me to dinner. When he got to the house, he sat me down in the living room and looked me in the eye. I wasn't sure what he wanted to say.

"Marc, what are your plans going forward? "You are due to graduate in a month and I don't want you sitting around the house on your computer, day and night. You need to do something with your life, before you completely lose your momentum."

I glanced at the rug. "Jack, do I even have the money to go to college? How am I going to pay for anything going forward? How am I going to get by?"

"I'm glad you asked. You've noticed that the lights and heat are still on here at the house? You're taken care of financially to go to college and money left over to start your after-school life." I took a breath of relief and continued to listen.

He continued. "I am your financial guardian and the executor of your parents' estate, which is approximately three million dollars after cashing in the life insurance and investments. So, you need not worry about that. There is enough to take care of you for the rest of your life without financial constraints. There may be more money in the future, as I will be filing a lawsuit on your behalf seeking damages and compensation for your parents' wrongful death."

Three million? I was stunned. It was more money than I could envision in my brain.

Jack pointed his finger at a family framed photograph on the wall. "Your parents loved you very much. They wanted to give you everything. They made me your guardian because they knew I would carry out their wishes for you. That's why I want you to go to college and not live off the money as a slug. I will not let you bum around living off your inheritance."

With a sigh I sadly said, "I am not ready to go to college nor do I have a desire to waste my inheritance on foolishness. I will attend college, but I need some time to clear my head. A year would be enough time to get myself together."

"What do you plan to do?"

"I want to get away from Cleveland and out of this house. I want to backpack through Europe for a few months, beginning in the spring. I'll visit museums and see the sights. I wasn't sure how to pay for it, but it sounds like the estate can give me what I need."

Stunned, Jack asked, "Where did you get that idea?"

"Mom always talked about how she and Dad went backpacking through Europe when they were younger and fell in love. I found their travel diary when I was rummaging through some boxes last week. If they could do it, so can I."

Jack looked at me, hard. I knew he was assessing what I said. He observed my short stature, skinny body, and the dark circles under my eyes from months of grief to determine if I had the fortitude to make the trip alone. He rubbed his fingers, sighed, and nodded.

"Okay, Marc. If we can compromise on an itinerary and make sure your passport is current, I will agree to fund your travels. A clean break and some time away might be the best thing for you. You have to promise to stay in touch by phone or text, so I know you're safe."

I told myself I wasn't running away from my problems. I just needed to find out who I was, away from school and Cleveland.

Chapter 4

Jack handed me an envelope of cash, traveler's checks, my health insurance card, and a credit card. On the envelope, he wrote down the addresses of the American embassies in each country I was set to visit. I used Mom's old scrapbook to plan my itinerary. I was planning to retrace the route my parents took after college as they explored Europe.

Jack put his hand on my shoulder. "Europe today is not the Europe your parents visited thirty years ago. It's a dangerous place to be an American. Keep your wallet closed and your valuables in your front pocket, watch your mouth, and be very careful with whom you make friends. Hide your money and your passport at all times."

"I'll be smart and careful," I promised.

"While you're gone, I'll take care of the house."

I took a deep breath. "Jack, sell the house and all the contents. When I come back from Europe, I don't want to come back to this place. There is nothing I want to keep. I see ghosts here and they haunt me."

I thought Jack would argue with me, but instead he nodded. "I'll save the family photos, a few things you may want years from now, donate the clothes and put the rest on the market. I will miss you while you're on your trip, kiddo."

With that, he put his arms tightly around me and held me until I could control my emotions again.

Chapter 5

Due to delay, my flight out of Cleveland didn't take off until midnight. I was wired and couldn't fall asleep as the anticipation and fear of the unknown kept me awake. As the city lights receded below, I envisioned breaking out of my shell. I knew this trip would change me, bring me closer to my parents, and help me become the person I was meant to be.

I prayed for the first time that I could remember. I asked for the blessings my parents had: "A life partner and lover who would cherish me for who I am. God, if she looks like Lisa, the head cheerleader, I will be forever grateful and I want to have real, true friends."

I reclined in my seat and closed my eyes. I was too excited to rest, but I floated through daydreams of the adventure ahead of me. I envisioned meeting someone on the train and, when we looked into each other's eyes, we would instinctively know we were destined to be together for eternity. The sky outside my window was an impenetrable black, I hoped it wasn't the color of my future.

After nine hours in the air, the flight landed at Heathrow in England. I staggered through the terminal, clutching my itinerary. All the signs were in English, which made it easy to find the West Coast Main Line, which would take me out of London to a town called Windermere. I bought a ticket and collapsed in my seat, holding my backpack in my arms. I was fast asleep before the train left the station.

Decades ago, my dad had traveled up the English coast to the Lake District National Park. I was following in his footsteps and planned to stay at an inn close to the park. When I arrived, it was exactly like my dad had described it twenty years ago. The inn was an old three-story Victorian building with a turret in front of its steep, heavily shingled roof. The wings and bays faced many directions. The outer house had been painted in earth tones: mostly yellows and browns, with accents of a soothing sea green. As I walked up the stairs to the wraparound porch, I saw the innkeeper. He was kneeling by the door, gripping a hammer in his right hand.

"May I help you, lad?" he asked. His gray hair and lined face looked hardened, as though the wind from the nearby lake had covered him in a silver patina. The edges of his mustache were tinged a rusty color, from either tea or tobacco.

I peeked at the itinerary I clutched to verify that I had the correct address, and then I introduced myself. He said his name was George Wills.

"Lucky timing," he said. "We are in the midst of a spell of unusually warm weather. The cold weather scares off most tourists this time of year, so you've got it virtually to yourself. Let me show you to your room. You can get settled in and we'll talk in a wee bit."

Inside, the house was quiet and packed with cozy furnishings that were over a hundred years old. Everything appeared comfortable and handmade. The walls were textured with patterned masonry. Oriental rugs were scattered across the stone floors.

As he led me upstairs, Mr Wills explained, "The inn has only six rooms. Breakfast will be served every morning between eight and ten. If you choose to take hikes through the hills, I have canteens to loan you. I recommend two or three sights, that are must-sees."

I dropped my backpack and took my shoes off as soon as I was in my room. There was a fireplace with a stack of wood beside it; in spite of the warm weather, he warned me that the nights would remain chilled. I looked out of the window at the beautiful, fresh English countryside. The lawn was dappled with brilliant yellow buttercups, and a kind of black-and-white bird I'd never seen before hopped across the field, hunting for bugs.

There was no telephone and no cell service, so instead, I scribbled a few lines on a postcard that I mailed to Jack. Then, I chose an old, leatherbound book from the bookshelf by the bed. I read until my eyes drooped and I dozed off.

I jerked awake to the sound of murmurs, heavy breathing, and muffled screams. The room was completely dark: it had to be close to midnight. The sounds were coming through the adjacent walls, possibly from the room next door. Was the inn haunted? I pulled the covers up higher. The moans were replaced by giggles, which faded into a dead silence. I closed my eyes. Just in case it was a ghost, I prayed for protection. Eventually, I fell back into a deep sleep.

When I woke up, my stomach told me it was time for breakfast. I dressed in hiking gear and went downstairs. The dining room had a few small tables decorated with formal tablecloths, real china crockery, and neatly folded cloth napkins at each place. I chose a seat close to the window. Near me at the next table, two women were sipping tea. At first, I didn't notice that they were holding hands. Like me, they were dressed for hiking, sporting loose-fitting, long pants rolled up at the ankles, brown hiking boots, heavy gray wool socks, long-sleeved shirts and red bandannas around their necks.

"We thought we had the place to ourselves," one of the women said, smiling.

"So, did I," I said.

"You're American," exclaimed the taller woman. She was muscular, with a cute figure, dark brown curly hair, and a harder-looking face. She tilted her head to the side and appraised me.

"I'm from Cleveland," I blurted.

"My name is Gabrielle. Cristina and I live in Kensington, a London borough. We are here on a short holiday."

Cristina smiled at me again. She had straight, medium blonde hair and a perpetually kind expression. Her cheeks were sprinkled with soft freckles. Physically, she appeared as athletic and well-conditioned as Gabrielle.

"Well, I guess it's just us at the inn," I said. "You two, me, and the ghost."

"What ghost?" Cristina asked.

"Didn't you hear any strange noises last night?" I asked. "This place might be haunted. I woke up last night and there was a strange howling then one of the ghosts laughed. It sounded like it was in the walls. Very eerie."

Cristina blushed. Her ears and neck turned bright red.

Gabrielle smiled and said, "I apologize if we disturbed your sleep. We assumed we were the only guests here."

I stared at her like a deer in headlights until her comments finally registered. Then, I blushed just as hard as Cristina. I was mortified. I tried to stutter an apology, but I couldn't find the words. They laughed, and then, mercifully, Mr Wills came with my breakfast tray. I ate my eggs and scone quickly, wishing I could disappear.

In spite of my awkwardness, the women invited me to join them on a hike to some of the park's lakes and waterfalls. I accepted their invitation with the biggest grin. I guess I hadn't been too nerdy with my comments after all.

Chapter 6

Mr Wills drove us to the trailhead in his faded blue Citroen Jumpy van. When I got out, I surveyed the green mountain range that we would be climbing. There were only a few spindly clouds in an azure sky, and the day was already warm and muggy. I was glad I'd borrowed a canteen.

"It will take us a while to ascend to the waterfalls." Gabrielle pointed to the mountain as she spoke. "The way down will be much quicker."

"The trail should be clear," Mr Wills said. He agreed to pick us up in a few hours and waved at us as he drove away.

We began our climb. There was still a little damp dirt trail. The area experienced recent spring rains, but the pathway was in relatively good condition. We hadn't walked far before Gabrielle spoke up and asked, "Marc, what brought you to England? Aren't you a little young to explore Europe alone?"

"I'm not a little kid," I said. "I'm a lot older than I look."

The women exchanged a glance. I still had a baby face, but I didn't feel young inside at all. Grieving had made me feel ten thousand years old, more ancient than the sun-bleached rocks that lined the trail.

I reluctantly told them. "My parents died about six months ago. They used to talk about how they visited Europe when they were younger. I wanted to feel closer to them and decided to follow their journey."

Talking made me forget that my calf muscles were burning, and the incline, or the harsh feeling building in my chest, caused shortness of breath as we gained elevation. The women walked up the mountain as easily as if it was a stroll in the park. Band practice marching didn't prepare me for a physical hike like this one. I trailed behind. Regardless, I decided to man up and pretend that I could keep up with them. Truthfully, I needed take a five-minute rest to put aside the mental cries of my body.

After a while, our conversation lagged, and I focused on the surrounding beauty. I'd never been anywhere this wild and untamed before. The trees displayed green leaves of spring while small purple and yellow flowers were interwoven into the trampled ground cover. The air was pure, sweeter than home. It was clean and soft with humidity. A heron flew over us, heading toward the lake. Small animals or birds rustled invisibly under the leaves. As we walked, I forgot about my burdens, my grief and just concentrated on God's splendor.

When we reached a plateau and stopped to drink some water, I asked, "What's your story? Why are you two here?"

Cristina glanced at Gabrielle and smiled. "We wanted some time together before our commitment ceremony this summer. Sort of a pre-wedding honeymoon."

I swallowed hard and thought, *"A lesbian wedding."* I tried to keep my voice from sounding shocked as I asked, "So tell me, how did the two of you meet?"

Cristina answered as she followed Gabrielle. "I was teaching sociology at King's College in London. It was the same old story: I was kissing frogs and hoping that one of them would turn into a prince. I could not find a man who had the intellect, moral character or a level of faithful commitment. None of my relationships lasted more than a semester. I knew I was attracted to girls but didn't really see myself settling down with a woman."

"My turn," Gabrielle interjected. "I had just broken off my engagement when I met Cristina. I am a nurse at King's College Hospital and my then ex-partner was a surgeon who I worked with. We had set a date, but a couple of months before the wedding, I found out that he was having a sexual relationship with one of my closest friends. I moved out the next day. I found an apartment near the university, in Cristina's building."

Cristina yelled playfully, "Okay, now it's my turn! I met Gabrielle as she was carrying her things into the flat next to mine. She told me what had happened with her ex, and we went out for a drink to drown her sorrows. Since we lived in adjacent units, we spent lots of time together. I couldn't tell if she was straight or bi. I figured nothing would happen, since we were both dead set on dating the worst guys we could find. Then, one night, she made her move. And here we are."

Gabrielle took Cristina's hand and said, "It started out so romantically. She was already my best friend before I fell for her. Naturally, we progressed to being lovers, and soon we will be married."

We walked for another hour, talking about the details of their wedding. Sometimes, they held hands or casually kissed, not seeming to care if I saw them. Finally, we reached a beautiful glacial lake, that was so cold that my feet tingled and went numb when I tried to wade in it. We sat near the water and ate lunch, relaxing. The lake reflected the royal blue sky and was as still as a sheet of glass.

The day was getting hot and we were low on water, so we decided to begin our descent back. I was caked in dirt, sweat and excited to return for a hot shower. I had envisioned galloping up the mountainside like an army ranger, but hiking was a lot more taxing than I anticipated. I knew I was the one slowing down the group. Gabrielle and Cristina could have easily gone on without me, or outpaced me, but instead they stuck close by and kept making conversation to pass the time. They teased me about putting ketchup on my sandwich and

41

laughed when I said I loved 'French fries' instead of 'chips'.

Gabrielle surprised me when she asked, "Do you prefer boys or girls?"

I told her. "I think girls, but I don't have any dating or firsthand experience to base my preference."

Cristina laughed. "Most of us were virgins at your age. In time, you'll meet that person with whom you will have relations."

I felt comfortable with them. For the first time, my virginity didn't feel like a stain. I was in Europe, walking through a pristine forest with two beautiful women. I was having the kind of experience I really sought.

The final leg of our hike was now across the slope to the Aira Force Waterfall. We stood on the centuries-old bridge, overlooking the cascading streams. Tons of water rushed down a hundred-foot drop into the pool below. The force of the water emitted a crashing sound which could be heard from the bridge and far down the path.

Cristina said, "Mr Wills told us that the bridge and waterfall have magical powers. He said the spirits who live here grant wishes. We should try to see if it comes true."

I took a few pennies from my pocket, and we each took one, kissed it, made a wish, and threw the coins down into the falls. I closed my eyes and said a prayer asking for future blessings.

I turned to my companions, but Gabrielle shushed me. "Don't say what you wished for, or it will never come true," she said.

I clamped my mouth shut. My wish seemed too lofty to ever come true, but who knows?

At the park entrance, we telephoned Mr Wills. He said he was on his way, so we waited for him. The exercising was exhausting but I was overwhelmed by all the beauty I'd taken in.

"You've got roses in your cheeks," Cristina told me. I smiled at her. For the first time since my parents left, I was truly in a good place.

After a meal at a pub, a shower, and some time lounging with the ladies on the inn's massive porch, I went back to my room. I left the lights off and watched the sun fade behind the mountain. Dusk crept in, softening the edges of the wallpaper pattern and the letters of the book I held in my lap. Finally, I climbed into bed. My legs felt warm and stiff. There was a gentle knock on the wall by my head: Cristina and Gabrielle, saying goodnight. Within a few minutes, I was fast asleep.

Chapter 7

I awoke with the morning light peeking through the old brocade curtains that adorned the windows in my room. I was putting on my shoes when Gabrielle and Cristina knocked on my door. They invited me to join them downstairs for breakfast.

"How did you sleep, ladies?" I asked.

Gabrielle said, "You make us sound so old. The 'ancient ladies' had a pleasant night."

I decided to try my hand at humor. "The ghosts were quiet, last night." They giggled.

"Marc, we planned to spend the day renting bicycles and tour the local shops and towns. Maybe we'll stop at a brewery. Would you like to join the old women?"

It was a perfect day for a ride. The sun was shining. The temperature was about sixty-five degrees and there was a slight breeze in the air. We rode bikes to the closest town and walked from one store to the next. My new friends were shopping for their new home, and chose several tablecloths, and small houseware items to buy. When I saw how happy Gabrielle and Cristina were, it made me wish I had someone to buy presents for.

These were the first two people who didn't treat me as a nerdy teenager. They were the most perfect traveling companions. I sensed that I was being nosy with my questions, but they were so different from anyone I had ever known. They indulged my curiosity and encouraged me to ask personal questions.

As we walked between shops, I asked Cristina about the wedding they were planning. "Is a commitment ceremony different from a wedding?"

"From a legal standpoint, yes. But on the outside, everything will look the same. We will exchange vows in the country church, in the parish where I grew up. The vicar who baptized me has agreed to be our officiant."

"He's such a kind soul," Gabrielle added.

"We will both wear wedding dresses and lace veils, and we will both walk down the aisle. We wrote our own vows, and we'll exchange rings. This holiday is kind of our honeymoon, since the new school term starts the week before the ceremony, and I have to work. We might try to plan another getaway in a year or so."

"That's right," Gabrielle said. "Paris is just a train ride away. It's easy to get jaded about it, when you've lived here all your life."

"Do you plan to have children?" I asked.

Cristina blushed, and I wished I hadn't asked. I apologized, but she shrugged it off.

"Your question surprised me," she said. "I don't mind telling you. We want to have a family, which means we'll select a sperm donor and I will get pregnant, since Gabrielle doesn't have the ability to have children."

"How many do you want?" Gabrielle asked, grinning at Cristina.

"Fifty," she joked.

"Is that all? How about just one healthy child?"

"One is perfect," Cristina said. "As long as they're as smart and nice as Marc."

They shifted the conversation to my program at Northwestern. Suddenly, college seemed more interesting. I told them how I created software, games and programs and taught myself coding all through high school. I shared how excited I was to be accepted into a software engineering program.

"Games are my obsession," I told them about my favorite games, the friends I played with, and how much it meant to me to have a place to unwind, kill a few dragons, and chat with my team. I explained all about my latest world-building project. They didn't look bored but asked all kinds of questions. I wasn't embarrassed or worried about seeming like a geek to them. I gushed, grateful to finally have something to talk about that didn't remind me of my parents.

When we returned to the inn, my friends hugged me. "Tomorrow we will be leaving for London early in the morning. So, let's have dinner together and say goodbyes." Sadness overcame me, because I would be alone again.

I didn't know it, but Cristina and Gabrielle had privately discussed how they could help me.

"He's a sad chap," Cristina had said. "With his parents being killed a few months ago, he's got no friends and practically no family. What if we invite him back to London and help him forget his troubles?"

Gabrielle kissed her and said, "You have a heart of gold. That's why I love you."

During dinner, Gabrielle handed me a card with her address and cell phone number written on it in pencil. "Next week, when you arrive in London, we want you to crash at our flat," she said. "The city's more fun when you have someone to take you around. We should make some memories together."

I was overjoyed. "Awesome!" I shouted.

Before turning in for the night, they hugged me again. I was thrilled with the prospect of visiting them in London. This trip was turning out to be even better than I had imagined it would be.

Chapter 8

Since I hadn't called Jack in a few days, I waited until it was morning in Cleveland and took my cell phone into the meadow on the top of the hill to call him. Mr Wills had told me that the only way to get phone service was overlooking the town. I didn't have any bars until I was halfway up the hill. I found Jack's name in my contacts and clicked on his number.

"It's me," I said when he answered.

"Hi, Marc," he said. "How's the British Empire treating you?"

I had started to tell him about my adventures, when I sensed that something was off. His voice sounded dull and preoccupied.

"What's wrong, Jack?"

"Nothing," he said. "It's early here."

"I can tell something is up. If the shoe was on the other foot, you would want me to be honest with you." I waited for his response.

"We had a little medical crisis, and Helen is going in for a biopsy tomorrow," Jack said. "I always get nervous before these things."

"I'll keep you in my prayers. I will call you in two days, so you can tell me Helen is fine," I said.

"I hope it will be that simple. They found some cancerous cells, in her blood work which suggested there is a problem. The doctors are confident that it is something that surgery and chemotherapy will cure."

"Please give her my love and let me know how it goes as soon as you know something."

He thanked me and asked about my trip so far. "I made friends with Gabrielle and Cristina, and they invited me to their place when I'm in London." He chuckled but wouldn't explain what was so funny.

"Marc, enjoy yourself, very few men have had two women. Sorry got to go, that's Helen on the other line." After he hung up, I checked my phone for a long minute, then put it back in my pocket. Gabrielle and Cristina were practically married and at least ten years older than me. I should have explained we were only friends.

From the top of the hill, I could see another nearby lake. It winked at me, throwing back the light of the setting sun. There was a golden mist over the water. On the far shore, I saw someone rowing in a long, lazy arc that traced the shoreline.

Suddenly, I experienced a memory of a long-ago summer vacation. My family visited White Fish Lake in Hayward, Wisconsin. As I gazed at the rowboat, I could hear my father telling me, "Worms do not talk, because they do not want to scare away the fish. Be quiet, Marc."

I had been such a pain in the ass. I complained that the mosquitoes were eating me alive. And the fish were eating my worms. I blamed the fish for knotting up my fishing line and complained that I was hungry. If my Dad didn't love me, he would have thrown me to the fish as bait.

I remembered my day had turned around when I caught some fish and the air became warmer. We climbed out of the boat with Dad carrying a string of perch that needed to be cleaned. When he was done, Mom pan-fried the fish with butter, along with potatoes.

I watched the rowboat glide across the English lake's slick surface, and I could almost hear my dad's patient voice as he untangled my fishing line for the millionth time. When the rowboat slid onto the beach, my memory was over, and the details of that summer vanished, spiriting my parents away to the distant past.

I staggered down the hill. At first, I didn't realize I'd been sobbing as I reminisced about the past. I wiped my face with my T-shirt and walked back to the lodge.

Chapter 9

Jack shared, "From what I remember, your Dad and Mom met up in England. They checked out a few castles and then traveled to Scotland. It was the '80s, so they probably experienced unusual lifestyles and cultures back then. They were young and thought they were rebels."

I struggled to imagine my parents with mohawks, tattoos or safety pin earrings.

Jack added, "They were experimenting then, just like you are now. When they came back to Cleveland, they were happy to settle down, satisfied with their American lifestyle."

"That makes sense," I said.

"I'm cooking tonight, since Helen is still recovering," he told me. "Wish you were here, Marc. Take care of yourself. Keep in touch. We love you."

Although the museum wasn't open yet, a small crowd of visitors gathered outside. I was glad I'd caught the early commuter train back to the city. I wanted to take my time inside the British Museum with its treasures.

My parents never took me to museums. We picked apples, blueberries and strawberries, attended baseball games, went fishing, and attended movies together, but cultural study wasn't their passion. I thought of them as I watched the attendant roll back the metal gate that blocked the entry to the museum. I walked up the wide stone steps with a handful of other tourists, entered through the thick metal doors, and made my way into the awe-inspiring hoard of cultural wealth.

After nearly a day there, I walked to the Tube and tried to visualize my parents on the same street, years earlier. What did they do, here in London? Did they experiment with sex or drugs? My parents were married after they returned and never again ventured outside the United States. I wondered why.

I found my hosts' address using my map program and noticed it wasn't far from the River Thames. It was a newer structure, with dark tinted windows held in place by steel girders. From a distance, it had the appearance that the entire building was made of dark mirrors, reflecting London back at itself.

I buzzed their flat from the lobby. Gabrielle answered. With excitement in her voice, she said, "What are you waiting for? Hurry up, we're on the tenth floor."

I'd come to the right place. They were as happy to see me as I was delighted to be with them.

Chapter 10

I took my shoes off in the hallway and left them next to a pair of hiking boots and a pair of canary-yellow sneakers. Gabrielle and Cristina greeted me with exuberant hugs. I felt like I'd known them forever; it was easy to forget we had met only a week ago.

As I followed them into the flat, my toes sank into the soft white plush carpeting. I heard Irish folk songs faintly playing from a hidden stereo. I had never been invited to a girl's apartment before, so I checked-out the pictures and possessions, taking in every detail.

"We've only been here for two months," Cristina said. "We're not really settled."

She led me to the window and pointed out a few landmarks: London Bridge, the river, and the Tate Modern. Then, she showed me the guest bedroom. The walls were painted peach and a matching peach colored tapestry hung over a fold-out leather couch that was made up with powder blue bedding.

"Feel free to use the dresser and closet," Cristina said. "We were hoping you'd stay for a little while, as long as it doesn't mess up your itinerary." I'd already made up my mind to stay for as long as they'd have me.

We sat together in the living room around a square, smoked glass coffee table. On it there was a candy dish and a framed picture of Gabrielle and Cristina, embracing. I helped myself to some candy from the crystal bowl. I was hungry.

"Cristina and I made a bet that your feet are the same size as mine," Gabrielle said, looking at me. "Let me see something."

Gabrielle went into the master bedroom and came back a moment later with a pair of black high heels. She handed them to me and said, "Go in the bathroom wash your feet and try these on."

They were snug but they fitted. "See?" Cristina said. "You two are the same size. I win the wager."

"Yeah, but can he walk in them?"

I stood up and wobbled across the rug. I felt like a baby horse at first, especially with the thick carpet, but after a couple of minutes I was able to maneuver without falling over. It wasn't that different from the march step we used in band.

I flopped back onto the couch and wiggled my feet at Gabrielle. "Nothing to it," I bragged.

The women gave each other a guilty glance and devilish smile. Then, Gabrielle asked, "Marc, are you still a virgin?"

I turned beet red, put my hand over my mouth as I coughed. Only a few days had passed since I shared my status with them. Before I could say anything, Cristina chimed in.

"We have a friend we want you to meet," she said. "We think you're just her type."

I glanced down at my feet. As Gabrielle described the situation, I began to get hot and bothered at the prospect of having sex.

She said, "We have a friend named Dandi who is looking for a hookup. She has several fetishes. First, she will only approach the sexiest woman in the room. Second, she is attracted to virgins or people who are sexual novices. And third, she likes boys dressed as girls."

Cristina said, "We've seen you walk in heels, and we think you can pass. If you say yes, we will make you look like a hot woman tonight. Are you up for it?" I was speechless and would do anything to have sex.

My friends giggled. "You're turning purple, Marc."

"I'm not transgender," I sputtered.

"Nobody said you were," Gabrielle said, tartly. "Trans women aren't cross-dressers. You'd still be a guy. We're not going to make you take hormones or get surgery. You are simply going to shave a little and wear some clothes."

"That's it?" I was mentally weighing the propositions of losing my virginity and dressing as a woman.

"We must style you and apply make-up. Cristina wants to pick out your outfit."

Cristina said, "Is that a yes, Marc?"

I smiled and shrugged, trying to hide my shock at the situation. "When in Rome, I guess," I said. "I'll do it. Let's have an adventure."

They both squealed with excitement. Gabrielle immediately snatched up her phone.

"Dandi, how are you, girl? I was calling to make sure that you're coming tonight to the club. We've got someone who's just your speed, and we're dying for you to meet *her*." My eyes widened.

Gabrielle continued, "She's visiting from America, totally new to the scene. Cute as a button. We're going to be fighting the cougars off, you know how they are with virgins."

Cristina focused on me and noticed my discomfort. She whispered, "Don't worry about it, Marc. This is going to be a lot of fun. Go take a hot shower and shave your legs up to your bikini line and then we can get started. School is in session."

"What's a bikini line?" I asked.

She giggled and took my hand. "I'll show you in the bathroom," she said.

I'd never been so simultaneously excited and frightened in my life. Cristina led me to the shower and turned it on. She handed me a fresh razor, shaving cream and pointed to all the parts of my body that needed attention: armpits, legs, crotch. I didn't have any chest hair, so at least I could skip shaving that. I felt a tight, hot feeling in my stomach as I contemplated the prospects of getting laid. After the shower and shave Cristina inspected and then handed me a fresh towel.

The guilt caused me to announce, "I'm not gay. I like girls."

"I do too," she said. "Don't worry about it, Marc. This is just a bit of fun."

"Are you sure this is a good idea? This isn't how we do things in Cleveland."

Cristina smiled and squeezed my shoulder. "Tonight, you get to see how the other half lives. You don't have to be Marc today you are now *Marci* instead."

She pointed at our faces in the bathroom mirror, which was clouding up with steam. Cristina had me sit on the toilet with a towel covering my private parts as she applied make-up to my face. She pointed to my face in the steamed-up bathroom mirror. I was surprised to see how my reflection was softened. My lips, which I'd been biting, were extra pink and my hair naturally curled. The make-up made my eyes appear larger and more defined. I was taken back because I was pretty girl.

"See?" she said. "Give Marci a chance. You might like her."

Chapter 11

You are going to have to learn these lessons quickly and remember what you have learned. Practice wearing high heels at the flat, so walking and dancing in them looks and feels natural. Be more laid back, laugh, and let your smile and eyes communicate your wishes, not your words. You need a manicure and a pedicure. Your hair should be styled. Your body language must be feminine and so must your walk. At all times, you must remember that you are a teenage girl.

My lessons started the minute I finished shaving. On our way to Harvey Nichols, a cool, hip and upper-end store in London, Cristina asked me, "Do you notice the difference in the way we are walking versus the way you are walking?"

I was confused. I didn't see any difference.

She said, "Watch me again. Girls walk with our feet crossing almost in front of each other. It makes your hips swivel, which is much sexier than this little march you're doing."

I looked down at my sneakers. I didn't feel sexy, but I tried changing my gait. I could feel my hips start to roll as my weight shifted from side to side.

"Marci has some swagger!" Gabrielle said. "Hand on your hip, sweetie."

I thought of Lisa, the gorgeous cheerleader back at my high school. How would she have moved? I imagined her confident, sexy walk, the way she used to stride across the football field like it was her personal catwalk. I moved my body the ways hers moved. My legs glided underneath me, crossing like a model's. I almost tripped twice.

Gabrielle and Cristina whooped. "Work it! Get it, girl!"

We walked into Harvey Nichols; the girls headed right to their favorite displays. I stood around, watching them pull hangers off the racks. In a few minutes, they each selected a small mountain of clothes and hustled me to the dressing room. I went into one of the rooms and closed the curtain. Yes, it felt weird. I was hoping that I would not be arrested; I was still in my street clothes, and if anyone found out I was a boy in the girls' changing area, the police might place me in prison or the mental ward.

Gabrielle flopped a padded bra over the changing room divider.

"Put this on before you do anything else," she said. "You need all the curves you can get."

I'd never touched a bra before, not even Mom's. It couldn't be that complicated, I told myself. After a few false attempts, Gabrielle told me to hook it up just above my belly in the front and slide the hooks to the back

59

before pulling the straps over my shoulders. It was weird until I got the first blouse on. I turned to the side, then to the front. Suddenly, my body made *sense*. All the things I didn't like about it, from my skinny shoulders to my tiny waist, perceived better to me. I put my hands on my hips. I was a nerdy-looking guy, but I could definitely be a hot girl.

"Come out and show us," Gabrielle said.

"Good looking wig," Cristina said, as I strutted out of the fitting room to a chorus of delighted shrieks.

We settled on a perfect outfit for the club: a bright yellow silk top, pleated leggings, the padded bra, and a skin-tone lace thong. Gabrielle instructed me how to tuck my penis under the thong. At the last minute, Gabrielle also added a long, dark gold scarf to my shopping bag. She showed me how to tie it in a pretzel knot to hide my barely noticeable Adam's apple.

Our next stop was the salon; Mrs. Wong's House of Beauty. A stylist washed my hair and shaped the wig we had purchased at Harvey Nichols. While she gently fanned my head with a blow-dryer, another woman filed and painted my fingernails.

"Brows, too," Gabrielle yelled out, from the pedicure station in the corner. She and Cristina were leafing through some gossip magazines while two technicians massaged their feet.

My stylist looked me over. "Definitely need to wax those, ducky."

She applied warm, amber colored wax to my eyebrows, upper lip, and cheeks. It was worse than ripping off a Band-Aid, but at least it was fast. I tried not to flinch, but tears came to my eyes.

"Beauty is painful," the stylist said, and steered me over to the pedicure chairs, where I joined my friends. I picked a marine blue polish for my toes. The manicurist applied a neon pink to my fingernails which made my slim fingers appear pretty instead of wimpy. The nail polish was as bright and shiny as freshly sucked candy. I wiggled my fingers, flirting with the girls.

The walk home was fast. Cristina kept covering my eyes every time we passed a plate glass window: no peeking she warned. Finally, when I saw myself in a full-length mirror, I didn't recognize myself.

At the flat, we munched on snacks while the girls bombarded me with more instructions. If I'd ever been curious about girls, I was quickly becoming an *expert* on all things feminine. It was much more complicated than I imagined.

"When you're introduced to someone, lightly touch their arm and air kiss their cheek," said Gabrielle. "No matter how boring they are, smile and act interested. Girls love it when you tell them their look is adorable, cute or darling. Don't compliment anyone unless you mean it."

Cristina instructed me next. "Tonight, we are going to our favorite lesbian bar. Some girls may come up and ask you to dance. Just be cool. We'll introduce you to

Dandi so you can get a look at each other. After she sees you, play hard to get. Smile and turn around to strike up a conversation with someone else. You told me your Dad taught you to fish. So, you need to tease the fish with the worm, right? Once the fish thinks the worm is leaving for another fish, the first fish strikes, and you'll have her hooked."

"I thought you said she would definitely take me home," I said.

"That doesn't mean you shouldn't show her an enjoyable time," Gabrielle said. "Flirting is about having fun, and the thrill of the chase makes it more exciting."

Finally, it was time to go out. I put a plastic cap over my hair, freshened up in the shower, and then sat on the toilet seat wrapped in a towel. Cristina hovered in front of me, putting on the final touches with the make-up brush.

"Close your eyes so I can work my magic," she said.

I felt my eyelashes being combed and the make-up applied to my eyelids. Soft bristles brushed my cheeks, applying contour and highlighter. Finally, Cristina's small, soft hand pulled me up. She told me to go put on my new outfit but be careful not to smear my face. I squeezed into the clothes and slipped my feet into Gabrielle's high heels. I could feel every part of my body. The pants squeezed my behind, the scarf made my neck feel long and elegant, and the shoes made me want to dance.

"All done?" my friends asked. They led me into their bedroom and positioned me in front of their full-length mirror. "Open your eyes, *Marci*."

I was speechless. I was confused. My reflection was that of a beautiful young woman. I discovered a different me. I could not believe the way I appeared. I touched my face as I looked in the mirror and was stunned when the girl in the mirror copied my gestures. My own mother would not know who I was.

My hands reached out to the girls and I pulled them toward me in a group hug. I thanked them for all that they had done.

"You're better than playing Barbie," Gabrielle teased.

"I feel like something is missing," Cristina said thoughtfully.

Earlier in the evening Gabrielle had pieced my ears and then inserted plain posts. She had me close my eyes as she iced my earlobes before sticking a needle through it.

Now Cristina examined my face and said, "Your appearance needs one slight change." Cristina gently wiggled a pair of fourteen-carat gold earrings to replace the posts. My ears felt hot and pink, but the studs twinkled and looked so pretty that I couldn't resist loving my new look.

After my friends were dressed, they took a picture of me as a keepsake. We caught a black hackney cab to the 'She Soho Club', on Old Compton Street. Inside the taxi, Cristina applied hot pink lipstick to my mouth and instructed me how to freshen it. The three of us entered the club with our heads held high. I copied Gabrielle and Cristina, making sure my appearance sent a clear message: I was the most attractive girl in the house tonight.

Gabrielle and Cristina's friends were waiting at the back tables. They flocked around us and showered each other with hugs and kisses. I was introduced as Cristina's cousin, recently arrived from the States. These women were professionals: lawyers, doctors, and entrepreneurs. Some had been married; some had children. I told them that this was my gap year and my college major would be computer software engineering.

While we talked about the gender gap in STEM, Gabrielle nudged me. She whispered in my ear, "Dandi has arrived. Look to your left. Do you see her over there? She's the woman in the red low-cut blouse."

I glanced over my shoulder. Dandi stood at the bar with a colorful drink in her hand. She eyed me up and down, in a way a woman had never done before.

Nervously I said, "Here she comes."

Without spilling a drop, Dandi sauntered over, kissed Gabrielle, offered her congratulations on the nuptials, and smiled at Cristina. She never seemed to take her eyes off me. Finally, she turned my way and asked Gabrielle to introduce us. She inched closer until her cleavage was practically brushing against my padded bra. I didn't know if I should look.

"What should I call you, peaches?" Dandi asked.

I shyly told her my name, "Marci."

"American girls are so cute," she said. We talked for a couple of minutes and then she walked over to greet some other friends.

I followed the girls' instructions of joining another conversation while sipping a drink. I casually glanced Dandi's way, smiled, and pretended that I was watching her. Then, I turned to talk to another lady. Just like Gabrielle said, Dandi immediately came back. She summoned me to the dance floor with her index finger.

As I followed her, I felt a wave of anxiety. I didn't know how to dance. How steady would I be in heels? I quickly spotted the other dancers and tried to mimic them. It didn't matter. Dandi moved behind me, put her arms around my waist, grabbed my ass, and gave my neck a warm kiss that sent shivers down my spine. I turned my face toward hers and reciprocated. Soon, she was wearing most of my lipstick. She pushed me over to the wall and kissed me with her hand touching my inner thigh.

"Tell your friends you'll see them in the morning," she whispered in my ear.

Gabrielle and Cristina were still partying when I slipped in beside them. "Dandi is taking me home," I said, blushing.

Cristina grinned. "Enjoy," she said.

I smiled back at them as Dandi led me away.

In the cab, Dandi stroked my inner thigh, which caused my tucked penis to demand space to expand. I reached inside my thong to make room for it. Dandi seemed pleased that she'd created an erection she could play with. The taxi driver took us across town, through the dark streets, and into a gated neighborhood.

"Do you want to be a pleasing lover?" she asked as she touched my penis.

I couldn't help but say, "Yes," in my highest octave.

Her smile turned wicked. "Males that delay their ejaculation are better lovers. The goal is to last as long as you can. Do you understand?"

I nodded but didn't have a clue what she was talking about.

Her crimson claws sank into my leg. "If I say stop, you stop, whatever you are doing! If I make noises or even scream, don't stop, no matter what. Do you understand?"

I stuttered, "Yes." Her words made me uneasy and scared. Why would she scream?

"We are going to have a wonderful time," she said. "Let me see you smile."

Nervously, I obliged.

We arrived at her row house, and exited the cab, and walked to her front door. She practically dragged me into the house. Dandi had barely closed the door when she threw her arms around me and locked her lips against mine. Her bedroom and king-size bed was our final destination.

I was exactly what she wanted. She was going to be my instructor, and I was very willing to play my part and undertake some hands-on learning. As the door closed behind me, Dandi said, "Sit here while I freshen up."

I waited nervously, wanting to have sex but fearing the experience. My heart was racing. I settled into Dandi's comfortable reading chair as my eyes began to wander. She returned wearing a ruby-red silk robe. I automatically stood up as she approached me. She started to make out with me and stopped, instructing me as my heart and penis were pounding, demanding for me to rush, but I complied with her directions.

The sensation of our tongues caressing each other was breathtaking. She undressed me on the bed. I willingly would have followed her into hell at this point. She reached for my erect penis. As my eyes closed to enhance the wonderful sensation, I felt warm liquid sucking on it. I glanced down and Dandi was orally pleasing me. I didn't know such pleasure could exist.

She stopped before I exploded. Her index finger and thumb squeezed my head until my shaft softened. Then, she disrobed. My eyes were trained on her breasts. I placed my mouth on her right nipple.

She said, "Slow down, be gentle, lightly touch and tease it. Don't concentrate on the nipple. Yes, that is more like it."

My shaft was hard again, hoping for a quick entry.

Dandi pushed the sheets aside, placed two pillows under her behind and lay down. I was going to pounce on her, but she stopped me short. She said, "First, there is foreplay. Gently and slowly play with my legs and thighs. Make love to my entire body. Afterwards, I want you to go down and with your tongue lick me."

She pointed to the spot where she wanted to be licked and touched.

She said, "Once you hear me make sounds you will know that I'm enjoying it. Put your index and middle fingers inside me and make this 'come here' motion. Be gentle but firm and don't stop until I tell you."

I watched as her eyes closed as I gently felt the contours of her body. I occasionally licked around her nipple and then retreated to another spot. As the pattern of her breath increased, I went down to lick her. Breathing heavily, she gasped, "My clitoris, lick her."

I changed my focus and continued following directions.

I never realized how quickly my tongue could get fatigued, but I continued while moving my inserted fingers. Her lubricated vagina made the entry effortless. I could hear her scream with enjoyment. I continued until she crossed her legs and begged me to stop.

She said, "That was wonderful. Now, come her and kiss me."

She pulled my penis toward her body and placed it between her legs. I couldn't wait. The warmth of her body's lubrication massaged my penis as I jack hammered into her.

"Slow down, you won't last at this pace," she said. "Start over again, much slower. No, slower. Yes, that's perfect."

I made slow, deliberate thrusts into her. I was finally having sex. I smiled as my breathing huffed out and my heart pounded. I didn't know how much longer I could last. Dandi stopped me, rolled me over, and climbed on top of me. This position caused the greatest friction and enjoyment. I gazed at the crease caused by her thighs being in a sitting position and her breasts as they floated up and down. Almost without realizing it, my penis throbbed, and I climaxed. I released a deep breath and smiled, privately congratulating myself on my accomplishment. I felt like a gold medal champion.

Dandi kissed me as she lifted herself off me. She returned with a warm washcloth and she asked me for feedback. I gleefully told her that it was the best thing I had ever experienced.

She said, "Excellent. Let's start again."

She played with my shaft and it returned to its erect self.

"This time, enter me from behind." She guided me in, and told me to move slowly and gently. I found my rhythm, and with her encouragement, shifted to deliberate, forceful movements.

She instructed me as I performed all night. We tried every position and technique that she desired. Before dawn, every ounce of sperm had been drained from my body, my penis ached, and I craved rest for my weary body.

Dandi kissed the top of my head. "You are a sweet kid. Get dressed and I'll call you a cab back to Gabrielle and Cristina's place."

Twenty minutes later, I took the lift to their floor, knocked on the door, and was greeted warmly by the girls. I must have looked like a mess; I was still carrying my borrowed heels and the wig in my hand.

"Look, Marci can barely keep her eyes open."

"Lie down, sweetie. We'll pump you for all the details when you wake up."

They tucked me into bed in the guest room, where I fell asleep immediately. It was close to four in the afternoon when Gabrielle kissed my forehead and told me that I needed to shower.

"We have another party tonight," she said. "You have to wake up so you can eat and get ready."

I moaned with happiness. "This is heaven," I said. "Dandi was amazing. Your girlfriends are the best. I wish I could be a lesbian."

Gabrielle laughed. "I'm glad you see the appeal! Now, go wash all that sex off and get ready for a proper meal."

"I can't believe you do this every day," I said.

"There's a reason 'gay' means 'happy', sweetheart. Get a move on!"

That night's party started in the private room of a posh downtown bar but, around ten p.m., we decided to go into the street and dance to celebrate the girls' union next weekend. The entire block was cordoned off so that people could mingle, drink and party in the open air. Cristina told me there were often hundreds of people on the street. I was physically exhausted from the dancing. I teetered in my heels and was already sweating through the sheer orange blouse from the late summer heatwave.

Someone had set up a DJ booth and stereo on the sidewalk and he was blasting music into the air. The girls danced with their hands over their heads, swaying their arms and hips. Cristina and Gabrielle led me into the fray, and soon I was dancing without a care.

Cristina pointed at me and shouted, "Are you having fun yet?"

Guys had tried to hit on me during the night. I gave Cristina a mammoth smile, as I pumped my fist in the air along to the beat. *This is the best day of my life," I thought to myself. "If I was a girl, life would be filled with friends and excitement."*

Then, there was a booming noise. The streetlights shattered, plunging us into darkness.

Chapter 12

Breaking news: London Bombing. Three suicide bombers targeted the restaurant district this evening. Police estimate that one hundred and twenty-three individuals were injured, and thirty-four known fatalities. The bombings appear to be unconnected with any terrorist group. No suspects have yet to be apprehended.

"Miss, are you, all right?"

Groggy, Gabrielle looked up at the man. She asked, "What happened? Where is everyone?" All around her, the pavement was wet with blood. Parts of human bodies, broken glass and debris were strewn everywhere in her visible sight. The smell of death was in the air. She'd woken up in a nightmare. Unfortunately, it was real.

"Miss, I'm going to help you, okay? Try to stand and I'll help you walk a few feet over there so the medical team can assist you."

The man held Gabrielle securely, placing her arm around his back. He helped her stand and walked her over the medical aid area. Gabrielle was too stunned to ask any other questions. Part of her understood that she was in shock, because she wasn't able to control her responses or reactions. She was just as helpless as the patients she treated at King's College Hospital.

A response team nurse cleaned Gabrielle's abrasions, bandaged her wounds, and gave her a bottle of water.

"Do you know your name?" the nurse asked.

Gabrielle nodded and repeated her name and address. "Where are my friends? My fiancée was with me a minute ago," she said.

"Don't you worry about them. We're making a list of everyone and helping people get home or make their way to the hospital. You are lucky your wounds are superficial. May I have a driver take you home? You're scraped up and probably have a concussion, but you'll be all right. If you don't hear from your friends, call the police station later this evening."

Gabrielle arrived at a dark, quiet and empty flat at five in the morning. She tried calling Cristina's cell, but it went straight to voicemail. Gabrielle took a shower, popped three aspirin, and fell into bed with her hand wrapped around her phone. She had no messages when she woke up. The first thing she did was call the police hotline number.

"I'm sorry, miss. We don't have those names listed," the officer at the switchboard said.

"Why would there be no information?" Gabrielle yelled. "Where's Cristina? Where's Marc? How hard is it to find two people?"

73

The officer said, "I understand. Unfortunately, there are individuals who have not been identified yet. You are free to come down to Kensington police station and review the photographs of the unidentified fatalities. We can also refer you to the hospital where many were taken if you're a family member."

Gabrielle took a deep breath that turned into a sob.

The officer responded sympathetically. "I truly hope you find your loved ones safely."

Although her head ached, Gabrielle forced herself to get dressed. She left the flat and hailed a taxi, telling the driver to take her to Kensington police station. Upon her arrival, Gabrielle identified herself as a bombing survivor, looking for missing friends. She asked to see the unidentified fatalities, praying she wouldn't recognize anyone. The officer led her down to the lower level. There, on a wall, were photographs of the victims. Each picture was secured to the wall with masking tape. Each photograph had a number on it.

As Gabrielle frantically searched the photos, her eyes fixed on a familiar face. Cristina's eyes were closed, and her blonde hair was soaked with blood. Grabbing her stomach, Gabrielle collapsed to the ground. Immediately, the officer ran over to assist her into a chair as she wailed.

"I have to make a call," Gabrielle babbled. "This is a mistake."

"I'm so sorry," the officer said.

"She was fine when we left," Gabrielle said. She couldn't seem to stop talking. It was impossible that the love of her life was gone.

"We'll contact her family, if you can give us the name of her folks and where they live," the officer said. "Do you need a referral for grief services?"

Gabrielle shook her head. Their wedding was a week away. They had their gowns picked out, the band, the salmon entrée, the place cards. This couldn't be happening. She felt a dense fog roll into her brain, deadening the officer's voice. She wished she could disappear into that fog, leave the world entirely. Only one thought stopped her; the need to find Marc.

His picture was not on the wall of the fallen, and that gave her hope. She was informed by the police that the injured had been taken to three hospitals, each equipped with trauma centers. One of them was the hospital where she worked.

She went back to the flat and opened Marc's backpack. Digging through his clothes, she found an envelope of cash with embassy and emergency phone numbers written on it. Marc had mentioned Jack in previous conversations. She saw Jack's name on the paper and dialed him with her phone. She was surprised when he picked up.

"You don't know me," she said. "I'm calling because there's been an accident. Last night, my fiancée and I were out with Marc and a terrorist bomb went off.

He didn't have his passport with him, so wherever he is, he's unidentified."

She heard Jack gasp.

"The good news is, I believe he is still alive. I am going to check the hospitals to see if he's there. I will call you as soon as I have more information."

Jack murmured, "Thank you for the call. Where did you say you met Marc?"

"A couple of weeks ago, I met him at the Lake District National Park."

"I see," Jack said. "I definitely appreciate your call. Please, call me day or night if you hear anything. Let me know if I can help. If he needs me, I can be on the next plane to London. Thank you again."

Cristina was dead. The wound to her heart was so fresh it took Gabrielle's breath away. She curled up on the living room couch, hugging her knees to her chest, feeling like a lost soul. Her body and brain were numb. She gathered her inner strength and told herself that she had an obligation to find Marc.

King's College Hospital was only a short distance away. The route was so familiar that Gabrielle could practically get there with her eyes closed. She entered the hospital parking lot and swiped through the employee entrance, showing her employee identification card to the security guard. She went to the admittance desk on the main floor. Her friend, Adele, was working the desk today.

"What happened to you?" Adele's eyes widened as she took in Gabrielle's injuries. Bandages and tape peeked out from the collar of her shirt, where she'd caught the worst of the blast.

Gabrielle shrugged it off. "I'm fine. Can you see if you have a John Doe, in his late teens, admitted late last night? He'd be on the terrorist attack injury list."

"Let me check." Adele turned to the computer. "We have two John Doe fitting that description. One is Caucasian, an adolescent male who was wearing women's gear. The other man is Asian, dressed in street clothes."

"That's him. Where is the boy dressed like a woman?"

She found Marc in the room Adele gave her, on the fifth floor, in the recovery ward. The elevator ride caused her mental anguish not knowing what condition she would find Marc in. Slowly she approached the room and peeked inside. She smiled and took a relaxed breath for the first time. Marc was lying in the bed in a green hospital gown, an IV in his arm. He was sleeping.

Gabrielle grabbed his chart from the end of the bed and gasped in disbelief as she read it. She shook her head. Tears flowed down her reddening cheeks. The chart stated that shrapnel wounds had nearly disemboweled her friend. Flying metal had damaged his testicles so severely that the doctors elected to complete an orchiectomy to stop the bleeding to save neural function and lymphatic vessels. His wounds in his abdomen and lower legs required surgery. His penis had noticeable damage. He had been luckier than Cristina, but not as lucky as Gabrielle. He survived, but with severe physical scars that would heal but never fade.

Gabrielle pulled up a chair by the bed and sat down to wait until he awoke. Marc stirred but did not wake up. She sat there for hours while he slept. Guilt overcame Gabrielle as she regretted that Marc would never be the same. If she hadn't dared him to go out as *Marci,* would things have turned out differently? Guilt squeezed her throat. She pulled out her cell phone and sent a text message to Jack: 'Found Marc. He is in recovery from numerous injuries requiring surgeries earlier today. He is sleeping and out of immediate danger.'

Jack responded: "Thank God he is alive. Tell him we are praying for him. I owe you a debt of gratitude. The evening news carried a story of the bombing. Tell me that no one you knew died." Gabrielle told Jack she had lost her best friend in the world.

He responded by saying: "There are no words that I can say to comfort you for your loss. We will talk soon."

Gabrielle turned off the muted television and wrapped herself in an extra blanket that she used to cover her shoulders and her legs. She closed her eyes and tried to remember the faces of her friend and lover.

Gabrielle looked towards the heavens and asked God, "Why me? "Why did I survive and why did Cristina have to die?"

Just as she was dozing off, she heard her cell phone's muffled ring. She would have let it go to voicemail if she hadn't recognized the number. It was Hilda, her mentor and surrogate mother. Hilda was a world-renowned psychiatrist who ran a health and wellness center in mainland Western Europe. The clinic specialized in providing care for individuals dealing with gender and sexual abuse related to psychological trauma issues. The center also included a surgical clinic, where patients could receive gender confirmation surgery.

Gabrielle whispered, "Hilda, I need to go someplace where I can talk. I am in a hospital room. Talk and I will listen."

The voice on the other end of the phone came through loud and clear. "I was so worried about you. I saw the carnage on the news. Thank God you are alive and unscathed."

"This last twenty-four hours have been a nightmare," Gabrielle said. "I need your help. I wish I'd called you right away. Cristina was killed and I'm here with a young man whom we befriended. He has suffered significant injuries. He lost his testicles, has numerous abdominal wounds and his penis was scarred. To compound matters he lost both parents about six months ago."

Hilda cleared her throat. "Before we talk about this young man, let's talk about you. How are you dealing with Cristina's loss? What are you feeling now?"

"Honestly, if it wasn't for this American kid, I would have chased a bottle of sleeping pills down my throat with a bottle of wine last night. Cristina and I were supposed to be together forever."

Sternly, Hilda said, "Gabi, we must spend some time together. Can you fly to the center this week and stay with me?"

"Hilda, you know I love you with all my heart." Gabrielle spoke the words in a tone that a grown child speaks to her mother. "But this boy has no one else. I can't leave him."

"My doors are always open to you. I have a few things to say. First, I want you to promise me that you will not harm yourself. If you get depressed or have thoughts of suicide, you will call me immediately!" Gabrielle promised she would.

Hilda continued. "Now, Gabrielle, give me the boy's medical history and analysis from your observations of him."

In spite of her grief and exhaustion, Gabrielle found herself slipping into clinician mode. She scanned Marc's body, relaying her assessment to her mentor.

"Male, just turned eighteen. He has not sexually matured and has yet to reach completion of male puberty. He's a late bloomer. He suffers from trauma caused by years of low self-esteem, teenage adolescence, and the sudden unexpected death of his parents. He has no siblings and no real family." Gabrielle took a breath and continued. "His parents' death left him in a depressed state. He could be an easy target for dangerous behavior. Prior to their death, he had no close friends and no romantic interests. By his own accounts, he preferred non-personal relationships. He is absorbed utilizing the Internet and socializes using video and computer games. Cristina and I became his first real friends after knowing him a couple of days. He looked to us for parental guidance."

Gabrielle stopped to wipe away the tears that began to bead in the corners of her eyes. "When Marc met us, we paid attention to him. This fed his self-esteem and made him feel important. To fill the void in his life, he transferred the devotion for his parents to us. We dressed him up as a girl; we arranged for him to have sexual intercourse with a friend of ours. We introduced him to our friends as a girl. He felt like a member of the group. Feeling a part of our group, as a female, he may have become confused as to his gender identity. Hilda, I am afraid for him. How should I explain to him the extent of the injuries he suffered when he regains consciousness? My fear is that when he learns the extent of his internal injuries to his manhood, he may become self-destructive. Help me. What should I say to him?"

Hilda said, "I am proud of you, Gabrielle. Your years working for me were not wasted. Even in your own state of crisis, you were able to give me a brief, thorough understanding of his medical and mental state. Let me ask you some additional questions."

After fifteen minutes, Hilda had a more defined picture of the situation. She said, "I understand the issues at work now. I see that you are self-identifying with this boy. You've experienced counter transference; his emotional reaction to your caring behavior has created an emotional response in you. Also, he is much like you were twelve years ago."

Gabrielle bit her lip and said nothing.

Hilda continued. "I too worry that the boy may be self-destructive. I would not rush with testosterone replacement treatments right away. You understand what will happen to his body without additional testosterone for any appreciable amount of time. However, someone in his condition may become suicidal. I am afraid that artificial testosterone or hormone therapy may cause aggression and increase his desire to harm himself. We need to walk a fine line here. Consult with his doctors. This boy may confuse your friendship with a sexual attraction. You must be firm and love him as a mother or big sister. Let him know the difference."

Hilda became a bit sterner making her next statement. "Gabi, you must call me if you experience further depression. You must promise me that you will not hurt yourself. I expect to see you soon. Bring the boy with you as soon as you can arrange it."

They ended the phone call. As Hilda hung up, she thought back to when she had first met Gabrielle. The clinic and surgical unit were in their infancy, barely in operation for a year. Gabrielle was young too, only sixteen years old. She arrived looking like a kicked puppy, afraid of her own shadow. She was suicidal and sexually traumatized by her father. Gabrielle stayed at the Compound in the clinic for a year before taking up residence with Hilda.

Hilda gave Gabrielle all the medical attention, affection and love she needed. After graduating from secondary school, Gabrielle returned and worked for Hilda as an assistant while attending the nursing college in the area. Their relationship changed over time as it grew from that of a doctor-patient relationship to that of a loving friendship. Gabrielle proved herself to be a capable and intelligent surgical nurse.

Gabrielle looked down at the hospital bed. In many ways, Hilda was right. Gabrielle did see Marc as she remembered herself twelve years earlier. She had subconsciously decided that she would become his protective mother until he could regain his physical and mental health. She would do for Marc what Hilda did for her, so many years ago.

The following morning, Gabrielle returned to Marc's bedside. He was still asleep so, before he was coherent, Gabrielle called Jack. She was less hysterical and more under control than she was during their previous conversation. Gabrielle described the medical and psychological issues now facing Marc. She described in great detail the type and extent of his injuries. She sought to reassure Jack that everything that could be done medically, would be done. Gabrielle promised she would stick by Marc's bedside until he was healed.

Jack thanked her. He said, "My wife, Helen, is in the early stages of radiation treatment for her cancer. I need to be with her as much as I want to be there for Marc. I'm always available by phone. If you need money or anything call me day or night. I wish I could do more."

"If any new issues arise, I will call you." She could tell from Jack's voice he was genuinely worried and stressed.

Jack ended the conversation. "Marc has an insurance card in his wallet which should cover all his medical costs. If the hospital or the doctors have a problem accepting the insurance card, let me know and I will make financial arrangements. I love Marc like he was my own and will do anything I can to help."

Gabrielle cleared her throat. "If there are any financial issues, I will have the hospital contact you directly. We will talk soon. I am praying for your wife, too."

Chapter 13

The sunrise signaled the start of a new day. Marc began to fidget, and his eyes partly opened. "Where am I? I'm thirsty," he said.

Gabrielle softly rubbed the side of his face, kissed his forehead and whispered in his ear. "You are in a London hospital. The doctors operated on you after you were hurt two nights ago. You need plenty of rest to recuperate. You are not yet permitted to drink because of the abdominal injuries. You can suck on ice chips, which should ease your dry mouth. Hopefully, later in the morning, the doctor will prescribe a liquid diet for you."

"What happened? How did I get here?"

"There was a terrorist bombing. You and many other people were injured. The rescue workers found you and immediately brought you here. I called Jack and told him everything."

Just then, the duty nurse entered the room. She brought in a small container of ice chips, checked Marc's vitals, and updated his chart. She was followed by the staff medical resident and a surgeon. Gabrielle had to laugh sadly. Who else but her two-timing ex would be at the door?

The first words out of his mouth were cruel. "Did you go from girls to young boys?"

"Harold, may I speak to you in private, in the hall?"

He couldn't be professional, but *she* could. Gabrielle grabbed Harold's arm and yanked him outside. She kept her voice to a whisper, but her tone was ferocious. The conversation lasted several minutes, after which time Harold's attitude changed. He'd cheated on Gabrielle with her best friend and humiliated her in front of all their work colleagues. The least he could do was make an effort to be a decent human being for ten minutes.

He examined Marc and asked him questions. "What is your name? Do you know where you are? Who is this woman? Now, I want you to follow the light with your eyes. Tell me when the light disappears as I move it side to side and up and down. Open your mouth and stick out your tongue."

Marc complied as he held his hands folded precariously over his stomach.

Harold clicked off his penlight. "I am pleased with your physical recovery. The incisions are beginning to heal. Do you have questions for me?"

"What surgery did I have? How soon can I leave? I'm hungry and I need something more than water to drink, maybe a Coke?"

The doctor laughed. "No soda, your stomach is too sensitive right now. You may begin a liquid diet of soups, juices and water. I will leave it up to Gabrielle to discuss the details of your condition with you at a time she deems appropriate. If you continue recuperating at this pace, you may leave the hospital in a week's time. We'll release you once your body is able to accept solid food and you have regular bowel movements.

"I want you to start walking as soon as possible, but do not overdo it! I want you sitting up and I want you to move around. I am reducing your pain medications. If the pain is unacceptable, we'll increase the dosage. I will return tomorrow to monitor your progress."

Harold wrote a few notes on the chart, avoiding Gabrielle's eyes as he left the room.

Bette, the head of nursing, was the next to visit. Bette and Gabrielle stepped into the corridor as Gabrielle had a favor to ask.

"I need a leave of absence," she said. "I am hurting. With my loss of Cristina and the emotional pain I am going through right now, I cannot effectively perform my job. I need time to recuperate. I am not sure if it will be weeks or months."

Bette, a friend of Gabrielle's, assured her that she would pull the required strings necessary to facilitate her request. She could take all the time she needed, and paid leave to go with it.

Gabrielle returned to care for Marc. She reached for two ice chips and fed them to him to ease his dry throat. "Marc, you are on a few pain medications. How do you feel?"

"I'm groggy and my privates are hurting. By the way where is Cristina?"

Gabrielle's index finger covered her lips. She hushed him. "I do not want you to talk," she said. "The feeling of pain is because you were in a bombing, a bad accident. You'll be all right, but you need to rest until your body is healthy. I called Jack, and he is concerned for you. If not for his wife's cancer treatments, he would be here with you. I need you to rest. Close your eyes and I will tell you a story."

Gabrielle started to tell a fairy tale. She remained silent as to Cristina's fate and did not have the emotional strength to tell Marc the extent of his injuries yet. "Did you know that a castle once stood where the hospital stands today? It was the southern castle in the days of King Arthur and Merlin."

Eventually, the story she concocted put Marc back to sleep. She kissed his cheek and sat in the chair by his bedside, reading a book. As she nodded off to sleep, she could smell the death and carnage from the street where it happened. Her brain flashed nightmarish visions of bloody body parts, spewed on the London streets. The memory of Cristina's bloodstained hair and horribly mutilated face haunted Gabrielle. The shock of the nightmare caused her to wake in a sweaty, fearful state. After countless attempts to sleep, she finally surrendered and decided that she would live on coffee for the next day or two.

Chapter 14

The countless days recuperating from my surgeries in the small hospital room were blurred because of my pain medications. I overheard a member of the hospital staff, but it seemed surreal, as if I was dreaming, only to learn later that Cristina had perished in the attack. I had no desire to listen to the rest of their conversation because their words only inflicted pain. I realized my world as I had known it had ended. I was too consumed with grief to comprehend the extent of my injuries.

During one of our many strolls down the noisy, busy hospital corridors, Gabrielle prepared me for news that I would soon be told. Her tone was motherly as she said, "Marc, the doctors and nurses are coming this morning to examine you and to remove some of your bandages. I need you to be strong. The only lasting injury that you suffered was the loss of your testicles. You can still live a long, normal life."

This devastating news, took my breath away. My mouth opened and my eyes watered. I stopped walking. I had no idea I had lost my manhood. I eyed her and asked, "What future do I have? Who will love a deformed man who is incapable of having sex? Why should I live?" The question in my soul was, "*Why should I continue to exist? For what purpose?*"

With a forced smile and positive tone, Gabrielle tried to reassure me. "You can still find your soulmate, get married, have plenty of friends, live a fulfilling life, and adopt children. You are young and it could have been a lot worse. In time, you will learn that there was a reason God chose you to survive."

I closed my eyes and wished that I had died then. "Gabrielle, please let me return to my room and sit there alone for a while." After she left me, I cried myself to sleep.

In my mind's view, I was leaving the flat and entering the grayish-blue cloud of the girls' bar. The women were dancing, yet I could not hear the music. I walked over to the tables and made small talk with a few of them and then, I turned my head when I heard a familiar voice.

"Marci, you are dressed very hip and hot looking tonight."

"Cristina! What are you doing here?"

"Your mother will be here soon. She and your father are finishing their bicycle ride."

Excited, I called out when I saw my mother coming toward me. "Mom?"

"Marci, you do look beautiful."

"Mom, how did you know that I became Marci?"

"Cristina told me everything. I know that you have some tough decisions to make soon. I support whatever you decide. I simply want you to be happy."

It seemed that they were fading away from me. I yelled, "Mom. Cristina, come back! Come back! Come back!"

A nurse patted my arm and brought me back to the real world, saying, "I am sorry to disturb your slumber, but I am required to draw blood and take your vitals."

My eyes were barely open, and my brain was foggy. I looked to my left. My yelling must have attracted Gabrielle's attention, who was now standing beside me with a watchful gaze. Over the next several days, she rarely took her eyes off me. She observed once or twice that I had physically improved, but my mental state had deteriorated. I seldom spoke and didn't want to talk about myself or the attack.

Gabrielle tried to console me, saying that she knew from her own experience that I was mentally searching for a safe state of being. It didn't make sense, but I appreciated that she didn't press me for what I was thinking. She shared that over the years she observed that her patients dealt with suffering differently. The key was to accept reality. I understood that to mean: *"As a man I would have no life."*

***

When I was nearly off the pain medication and able to walk normally, Gabrielle called Jack. She updated him on my condition and offered him a solution.

"Jack, I want your permission to take Marc to the Health and Wellness Clinic in Europe. Doctors Hilda Frankel and Alexander Dolinsky are world renowned psychiatrists who co-founded the clinic. I will be texting you their phone numbers when I hang up. They are waiting for your call. I think it would be immensely beneficial to Marc to undergo intensive psychological care."

"What's his mental state at this time?" asked Jack.

"From what I have gathered, since the death of Marc's parents, he has had low self-esteem. Cristina's death and his other physical injuries have overloaded his brain with trauma, much like an electrical circuit with one too many appliances running at the same time. He needs to get well and find a happier state of mind. A regimen of exercise, meditation and therapy will help him. I believe there is no better place in the world for Marc, than this clinic. They will help him recover from his mental injuries."

Jack responded, "It must be worse than I envisioned."

With reservation in her voice, Gabrielle continued. "Marc woke up yesterday asking for people to call him 'Marci.' He wanted to be robed and referred to as a female. The hospital doctor agrees that Marc needs psychiatric care. He is depressed. He is seeking to escape his life and we believe he could be suicidal. Please look into the clinic. I will keep you informed on how Marc progresses here. I continue to pray for Helen's recovery. I will call you with updates."

Jack sighed and said, "Thank you." She heard remorse in his voice.

***

Gabrielle ended the call, walked into my room again, and put her hand on my hand. She said, "Friday, after Cristina's funeral, I plan to take you with me on the next available flight to the Health and Wellness Clinic. I discussed it with Jack, and he agrees it's the best place for you to recuperate. I will tell you more later. For now, I want you to rest."

***

The next day, Gabrielle telephoned Jack again and shared what she'd learned from a few conversations with various doctors. "I was hoping that the gender issues would resolve themselves," she said. "They have only gotten more pronounced. He thinks he is or wants to become a female. He has refused testosterone injections, which is a good thing for the time being, and is still suffering from trauma and depression. The professionals are afraid that, unless Marc receives psychological treatments, he could be dangerous to himself. Marc has agreed to go with me to the clinic we talked about yesterday. Do I have your permission to take him there?"

"Gabrielle, I have to be honest and tell you that I am out of my element with medical decisions of this type. I trust you, and you are thinking of Marc's best interests. I called the doctors at the clinic and they were impressive. Please keep me informed." Jack's voice was noticeably sad as he hung up the phone.

***

I couldn't go with Gabrielle to Cristina's funeral, so she showed me the pictures she'd taken of the memorial service. A horse-drawn carriage carried Cristina's remains to their final resting place. In her casket, Cristina was dressed in her white wedding dress. Her mother wore her favorite pink dress, the one that she'd planned to wear to her daughter's wedding. Gabrielle tightly held Cristina's parents' hands as they watched the coffin being lowered into the ground. She showed me a photo of Cristina's marker. Like Gabrielle, I cried.

"You're all I have left, Marc," she said.

"Marci," I said. "I want you to call me Marci."

Chapter 15

The only thing I remember on the way to the clinic was that the last leg of the journey was in a white Mercedes taxi with leather back seats. I have no other recollections. I was self-absorbed in my physical and mental pain and remained silent during the ride. I exited the taxi with a few essentials in a small piece of luggage. I stared at the imposing buildings in the middle of rolling green hills and walked into the building with Gabrielle's arm around my shoulder, as she occasionally hugged me.

I wore a T-shirt, a pair of loose-fitting gray stretch pants, and sandals. Gabrielle checked us in downstairs at the registrar's office. The young, French, female attendant asked us to wait in Doctor Hilda's reception area outside her office until she had completed patient rounds. Her hand directed us to a worn leather brown couch.

The clinic was commonly referred to as the Compound by both guests and staff. The older building had survived in the countryside where two world wars had been fought. It received its nickname during World War II, because it had been used as the regional headquarters of the Nazi SS. This solid, brick, four-story-high building housed guest dormitories. It was coal-heated in the winter, with no air conditioning in the summer.

The newer buildings had modern amenities, consisting of two floors, with natural gas heating and air conditioning. The two buildings were attached by connecting hallways. The administrative offices of the clinic, the spa, the resort guest lobby, therapy and exercise rooms, dining areas were in the newer buildings. There were eating facilities and exercise rooms in the older building for patients. But we weren't called patients here. We were called guests.

The clinic had a center for wealthy individuals who simply wanted to lose weight and maintain their physical fitness. There, they could avail themselves of the spa treatments while being pampered. The resort was perfectly located near the mountains between France and Belgium, offering both winter skiing and summer hiking.

The Compound provided its patients and guests choices of classes in yoga, tai chi, dance, nutrition, and wellness education. A renowned, French chef, prepared gourmet meals for the guests. An understudy French chef, cooked meals for guests. It was a perfect mountain retreat, both for the healthy and the impaired.

Hilda finally joined us in her office where we were waiting. She said, "Good afternoon. I was expecting you earlier, but I am very pleased to see you both." She gave Gabrielle a warm loving embrace and kissed both of her cheeks. Warm gray eyes peered at me over a pair of bifocals. As Hilda lowered her head she said, "And you must be Marc."

I immediately yet politely corrected Dr Hilda. "My name is Marci."

In a soft but firm voice, unfazed by my interruption, Hilda continued to speak. "Marci, I want to explain to you how this clinic works and how we work with our guests. We help people better understand the psychological issues they have so they can live normal, healthy lives. With this knowledge, they can make an informed lifestyle decision once they leave our care. To recover you must be physically and mentally healthy. Everyone (meaning the guests) is required to work, exercise, meditate, and eat a proper diet. These are the keys to opening the mind and correcting your issues. All our guests participate in individual and group therapy sessions. You will be expected to make your bed daily, clean your room, and be properly attired each day. You will be expected to dress according to the gender that you envision yourself. You may revert to your male identity anytime you wish. You may freely decide to remain a male and no one will question your decision." Hilda paused and waited for me to ask questions.

When I didn't speak, she continued, "We expect our guests to be respectful and courteous at all times. You may wish to become a young woman. If the doctors are assured that this is best for you, we may prescribe estrogen, a female hormone. This hormone will allow you to develop female breasts and aid in the redistribution of your body into a female shape over time.

"There is a story about the American actress, Katherine Hepburn, who wanted to be a boy. In fact, she asked people to call her Jim. One day she realized that she was in the right body and she was happy to have been born a woman. I am telling you this because some young people reconsider their choices as they mature. We are reluctant to institute permanent changes to our guests unless we are assured that it is the right solution for that individual.

"Nearly eighty per cent of all teenagers wishing to change their genders wake up one day and change their minds. Yet, fewer than three per cent of people who elect to have gender-related surgery express regret over their choices. Change is a normal part of maturation. Of the individuals who do go through the transgender experience, many of them hope that their lives will be different and happier. But many, after their gender rebirth, and after having completed the gender reassignment surgical process, do not find the contentment they had hoped for. There is a high percentage of transgender people attempting suicide. I suggest that has more to do with the world's limited understanding of gender, than with the individual's feelings about their choice to live authentically."

Hilda noticed my eyes were directed out of the window. "Here at the clinic, we take a holistic medical

98

approach and assume that psychological problems have roots. We dig out those roots and analyze them with you. Once you and your body are healthy, then you can make the appropriate life decisions."

Finally, Hilda turned her attention to Gabrielle. "Gabrielle, you will resume your position as a nurse at the surgical hospital. You will work three twelve-hour shifts a week, from six a.m. to six p.m."

Gabrielle smiled and laughed lightly as she listened to Hilda's words. "You haven't changed at all," she said, happily.

Hilda continued, "On Tuesday, Thursday and Saturday, when you are not working your shift, you will attend yoga classes and be a group leader in our patient therapy sessions. You will have an individual one-on-one therapy session with me every Monday and Wednesday evenings after work. You will also need to fit three cardio workout classes a week into your schedule. Any questions?"

"No, none."

Hilda turned and faced me. "Marci, I have been told that you are some sort of software computer expert. This facility needs to have their computer systems upgraded and implemented with various types of software protections. You can work three afternoons a week on this project. Two mornings per week, you will attend yoga classes and two days you will attend Pilates classes. We will provide yoga attire to wear. After class you will proceed to your therapy session. You will attend two individual therapy sessions a week and you will have two group therapy sessions a week. After therapy, you will shower and proceed to the lunchroom where you will eat. After lunch, twice a week, you will attend French language classes, French cooking classes, make-up, and voice training lessons. You will have behavioral training and lessons about how women handle situations and interact with each other. On Wednesdays and Saturdays, you will be expected to work in the kitchen assisting the chef with feeding the spa guests." Hilda took a breath. I was stunned. *"Was this the answer to my well-being or prison?"*

Hilda asked, "Marci, do you have any questions? I will have a written schedule placed under your door before you go to sleep this evening. Set your alarm to wake up at six thirty a.m. tomorrow and every morning thereafter. Sundays, we permit our guests to sleep late; a nine a.m. wake up call."

I stared at Hilda, seeing her for the first time. She was a tough, no-nonsense older woman. She was attired in a white blouse, black skirt, and the sensible shoes worn by nurses. As she spoke, she smiled. Her words sounded like orders to me. I wondered if I was sentenced to a prison which pretended to be a wellness clinic. Hilda asked me to step into the hall for a moment. I left, closed the door behind me, and returned to the waiting room. I heard Hilda's words but could not focus on what she said.

***

After the door closed, Hilda turned to Gabrielle. She said, "She will dress as a girl and we will treat her as a young lady. Possibly, she will want to rebel and seek to revert to living as a male. I hope my words today left her with doubts. Maybe if she sees the hardships women face, she may find that the grass is not always greener on the other side of the fence and she may choose another course. Most importantly, you need to make sure she understands the boundaries of your relationship.

"You too, need to observe those boundaries. Your mind is going to seek out a new lover to replace Cristina. If you have or experience sexual desires for Marci, you must control them. Each of you have suffered a loss, and it is only natural to seek out someone to replace them. Many times, therapists and patients confuse their relationships. You can be Marci's friend and older sister. No more than that. Do we understand each other? When was the last time you slept?"

Gabrielle snickered. "Sleep? When I close my eyes, Cristina's bloody body appears in my brain. I cannot sleep for more than an hour or two at a time."

Hilda's tone changed, and her voice became compassionate. "Tonight, I will have Gwen show Marci around. She will assist Marci with her room, organizing her things and where to go in the morning. I reserved your old room for you, and now it's time to go to sleep.

101

If you need a hot cocoa as a sleep aid, go to the kitchen and grab one. I will stop by in an hour to see how you are doing. Set the alarm, so you will not be late for your first day of work tomorrow."

***

Both Gabrielle and I were assigned to rooms in the clinic's original building. We were on the same floor but at opposite ends of the corridor. I walked down the hallway to my room and observed the weather-beaten wood paneling. The strips reached halfway up the walls against yellow plaster, which reached to the ceiling. The floors were made of stone and the only light came from ancient fixtures with yellow lights dangling from the twelve-foot-high ceilings.

As I entered my room, I felt a chill. The four walls were bare. The heavy, ugly, brown-stained, dusty curtains hid drafty, leaky old wooden windows. I moved the curtains aside and observed green rolling hills covered by tall, wild grass and colorful wildflowers. So many hills. That's all my eyes could see. I stared out the window for several minutes in the hope that Julie Andrews would come sprinting over the ridge singing, like in *The Sound of Music.*

In winter, the heavy curtains were the only defense to keep the cold air from entering the room. The stone floors were constantly cold. According to Gabrielle, in summer, the floors felt refreshingly cool, but in winter, the floors made getting up and getting dressed challenging. Each room was adjoined by an attached half bathroom, with only a toilet and sink. Showering facilities were located at the end of each floor. The shower stalls were separated by individual modesty panels and moldy plastic shower curtains for privacy.

As I was acclimating to my new surroundings, Hilda was in Gabriella's room. There she tucked her into bed like old times. Laughing, Gabrielle said, "You and the Compound will never change. Hilda, I am happy to be back if for no other reason than to see you."

Hilda kissed Gabrielle's head and then they hugged, wishing each other a good night and sweet dreams.

Chapter 16

It was the first group therapy session. I listened to the other three members as they discussed their lives in guarded ways. How could I discuss my feelings, when I didn't know how I felt? The numbness remained. Besides, why would I want to share my life with complete strangers anyway?

I listened and learned from their testimonies that each of them had faced a life of hell before coming to the clinic. As a last desperate measure, they were brought here.

One of the members was a French girl named Fiora. She was seventeen. As a high school student in France, Fiora came out as a lesbian, though she had never had relations with either a boy or a girl, and disapproving boys gang raped her.

John was seventeen or eighteen years old. He resided in an area outside of Wales in the United Kingdom. John was abused by his father and he was gay. His classmates rejected him and he had difficulty in social settings. He failed in school, causing him to become a frustrated individual who would regularly lose control of his temper.

Charles was high schooler from London. Charles suffered trauma after his parents divorced and his mother committed suicide. He came home from school one day to discover her body. He refused to share with us the manner of her death. Charles was a non-conformist, unwilling to follow rules at the Compound and became outraged when told he had to adhere to directions.

On a typical morning, I attended meditation, stretching, or Pilates classes. I wore body clinging, orange or black yoga outfits and short pink socks. Sometimes, I simply went barefoot to yoga. The exercise instructors did their best to motivate the four of us. Not being a morning person, it was difficult for my body to function so early. In time, I would come to treasure morning exercise and mediation classes because it cleared my mind to start the day.

Depending upon the day, I attended either group or private therapy sessions. My assigned therapist was Alicia. She initially asked me simple, non-threatening questions to break the ice. "Marci, how are you feeling this morning? Do you have thoughts that you would like to share with me? Do you have any questions about the program or your classes? How do you enjoy your stay, so far?"

For the first couple of weeks, I had nothing to say. To break my silence, Alicia suggested breathing and meditation exercises. She began every session with this regiment. After two weeks, I began to warm up to Alicia. She was no longer a stranger.

Each of us knew that we were here to overcome our issues, otherwise we would not be here. It took days for us to communicate with each other and, when we did, it was not necessarily civil. The two guys had done much of the talking. They were both alpha males, paranoid and had to be in control.

I had several brief conversations with Fiora. She was cordial but socially distant. She had beautiful olive skin and an hourglass figure that I envied. I found her physically appealing. Her dark, silky long hair hung below her shoulders.

I had been living in the Compound for several weeks. One night, while I was sleeping, I felt someone playing with my penis. It felt great. I woke up with a loud gasp and sat up, realizing it was not a dream. I had been sleeping naked and when I opened my eyes, I realized that Fiora was undressed in my bed. She'd climbed under the covers to be with me.

"Oh no!" She was freaking out, and had trouble breathing after she discovered that my testicles were missing. My initial instinct was to have the two of us sit up, as I hugged her. Then, I encouraged Fiora to join me in performing breathing exercises until she was able to control her shock. Embarrassed, I covered my penis with the sheet as we stared at each other.

Minutes later, one of the orderlies entered my room and calmly asked, "Fiora, please dress yourself, immediately. You must return to your room. You both need your sleep to fully participate in tomorrow's activities."

In my individual session the next morning, instead of Alicia, Hilda was sitting in the therapist's chair. She addressed me in a delighted voice, praising me. "Marci, I want to thank you for not having intimate relations with Fiora last night. Her problems have caused her to take excessive risks and perform unsafe sexual practices. This is related to her experiences in France."

I blurted, "The last thing I want to do is to hurt someone else. I have thought about hormone therapy and I wish to move forward with it. These last several weeks, I've decided to take the next steps on the road to be a real girl."

Hilda nodded. "I will consider your request, but you need to help me. You are the only person so far that Fiora has exhibited any desire to be friends with. Please befriend her, but you must be careful. Remember what I have already told you in confidence about her past."

An hour later, I sat with Fiora at the lunch table. We smiled at each other. I broke the ice by asking her to show me how she applied nail polish to her toes during our free time.

She responded, "I would enjoy teaching you. It will be fun. I'll see you tonight, in your room."

After lunch, I started my computer assignment. My initial task was to familiarize myself operationally with the current software versions and hardware systems that the clinic utilized. I began mapping out which individuals had access to which computers and software. Then, I analyzed how often the software was actually being used by the staff. After mapping the systems for both the hardware and software, I sat with Hilda and one of the office administrators. I pulled out a diagram of their computer system and a list of all their software programs.

I asked Hilda to review the diagram and continued to press her. "This is what you have currently. What programs do you need? Finally, what tasks do you wish to accomplish with your software? What are you unable to achieve on your current system that you want to improve?"

She was impressed by the depth and logic of my questions. Her answers offered me a good place to start for the project. We met several times each week until I had a complete understanding of their computer system and software needs. I made them aware of the potential financial costs of this project and received their approval to move forward.

Over the next year, my information technology skills improved. The practical experience was priceless. Daily, I spoke to the world's best troubleshooters from Microsoft, Google, Cisco and other IT companies. Together, we created solutions for the Compound's needs.

I flew to Israel and sat down with the top technicians from Checkpoint Software. They helped me develop programs and procedures to prevent hacking and virus software attacks. The more I learned, the more I wanted to learn. I now dreamed of attaining a position at one of the top companies. But first, I had to finish my female journey and then college.

The therapy sessions and the overall program stressed living a healthy life and maintaining a vocation. Together, each graduate grew in confidence that they could overcome their past trauma. Most returned home and were able to fulfill their potential.

Fiora worked in the infirmary. Because of her work, she became acquainted with medical terms and procedures. John worked in the accounting department. He trained and performed bookkeeping functions at the Compound. Hilda considered each of our individual talents, abilities and temperament when she assigned us tasks.

Once one group graduated, anther group was there to fill their beds. There were close to eight groups at the Compound at any one time. As the alumni had their suitcases in hand, Hilda hugged them and wished them success in all their endeavors. She provided each of them with the names of reputable therapists in their towns and a personal handwritten note encouraging them in their journey. I learned that a number of alumni chose to revisit the Compound every year, for a period ranging from a week to a month. They found that a regimen of exercise and meditation was beneficial in maintaining a happy home life.

My group graduated. I was the only remaining member still at the Compound. I was a late bloomer, slow to change. Hilda reassured me that I was working at my own pace, and I had plenty to process. As I continued to come out of my shell, my bond of friendship with Gabrielle intensified.

One evening, Gabrielle came for a quick visit. She had been working long hours. She felt underappreciated and needed to blow off some steam. The 'quick check-in' lasted over an hour. Once we started talking, there were many things we wanted to share with each other. We had become each other's best friend. Midway through our conversation, Gabrielle pulled a small box from her pocket.

"By the way, I have been holding on to these since you were at the hospital. I think it's time for you to wear them again."

I looked down and smiled. The diamond earrings that Cristina and Gabrielle had let me wear my first night out shone in her right hand. Without a word, she gently placed them in my lobes. A good, warm feeling came over me as I stared into the mirror.

Gabrielle asked, "Do you want to join me in town Saturday night?" I was caught off guard and didn't know what to say.

Before I could respond, she looked at her watch. "Oh no! I spent too much time talking to you again. I am late for my next scheduled session. Hilda will have my head."

I yelled to Gabrielle as she ran down the hall. "I can't wait for Saturday night! You are the best."

When I initially met Gabrielle, I would never have pegged her as the warm, maternal type. Like a piece of cactus fruit, her insides were sweet even though she had a thick and prickly exterior. Like my mother, she enjoyed tucking me into my bed and kissing my forehead at night. She was my best friend, sister and mother rolled into one person. I was truly blessed.

The next morning, Gabrielle reluctantly telephoned Jack. She was finally exiting the fog of her grief, and she was ready to confess the complete truth to him.

"How's the treatment going?" Jack asked.

"It depends on how you look at it," she said. "As I have shared with you before, Marci as she prefers to be called, demands to medically transform into a woman. I must admit that it's my fault. I feel guilty about it every day."

"What do you mean it's your fault? I talked to Marci, and she seems happy. She is an adult who can make her own choices. It's hard for me to get used to calling her 'Marci,' but I will respect her wishes."

"This isn't a typical coming-out story, though. Cristina and I dressed Marc up as a girl so he could have sex with a female friend of ours." She thought she heard Jack chuckle but continued with her explanation. "The next night, the night of the attack, we dressed him up again. As a girl, he found himself popular and beautiful. He admitted to us that he felt sexually confused. We treated him like a Barbie doll, and now he's forever changed."

"Don't blame yourself. You didn't set off the bomb. The identity questions and confusion must have existed long before the attack. Marc must have had these feelings before he met you. Believe it or not, most people have a cross-dressing experience or two in their lives. Yet, we don't all go for surgery and hormones. In college, I joined a fraternity. I had to endure an initiation process known as hazing. During rush week, I was told to dress up like a girl for three days and attend classes that way, in a dress and a wig. I had to shave my legs, put on make-up and wear a bra stuffed with socks.

"For an entire semester, students ribbed me and called me 'Jacquelyn'. I never found the experience enlightening and I never wanted to become a woman. I was born a guy and I'm going to stay one my whole life. Obviously, Marc learned something different from his experience. You didn't change him. You are simply part of his journey."

Jack added, "I'll talk to you and Marci soon. You did not cause Marc's injuries or your friend's death. There was nothing you could have done to change the course of destiny. I think you are one of the most compassionate individuals that I have known. I hope we will meet face to face in the future, so I can properly thank you."

Gabrielle hung up and choked back her tears. Jack gave her the absolution she desperately wanted to hear. *Finally, she thought. Maybe I can begin to let myself heal.*

Chapter 17

Four months earlier, Fiora visited my room with a box filled with an assortment of lacquers. She had a massive, multicolored collection of polishes, emery boards, cuticle tools and nail polish remover. I wore a blue tank top and a pair of dark blue running shorts. Fiora was braless, dressed in gray basketball shorts and cut-off T-shirt. She opened the small backpack she carried on her shoulder and pulled out two textbooks, a notebook and her manicure supplies.

"While I am here, I am also completing my high school course requirements so I can graduate. Hilda suggested you may be able to help me with math and science. I am having so many problems!"

"Sure, I would love to help you. Tell me, what problems you are having."

"The teacher speaks so quickly, and I have difficulty converting her words into French."

We went over to the desk and started reviewing her homework problems. She taught me the words in French, and I explained it in English. She was a quick learner. After an hour of math, we relaxed as we cleaned and filed our nails. Then we took turns applying nail polish to each other's fingers. After our nails dried, we returned to Fiora's homework.

When we needed a break, we got a basin and soaked our feet in hot water until they were soft. Then we applied lotion and polished each other's toes.

We transitioned from homework to girlish pleasures until late in the night. I hadn't giggled or laughed like that in my life. By the end of the night, Fiora had a solid grasp of her homework as we developed a bond of friendship. It was past curfew, but strangely, no one interrupted us.

Fiora began speaking to me daily in French. Initially, it was difficult to comprehend everything she said. Gradually, I became proficient enough to carry on conversations. After a couple of months, the understudy chef complimented me. He said that if he didn't know me, he would think that I was a native French speaker.

At the lunch table, I occasionally sat behind Fiora and braided her hair. With envy, we looked at glamour and fashion magazines for the latest trends wishing we had those clothes.

The next evening, Fiora came into my bed sometime after midnight and crawled next to me. As she did, she woke me.

"Why are you here?" I asked.

She held me tightly from behind. When I turned to look at her, her face was as white as a ghost. She was trembling and visibly frightened. I tried to remain calm, so as not to exacerbate the situation.

"Tell me what's wrong?" I urged.

Her lips quivered. "I had a nightmare."

I coaxed her to tell me more. She kept shaking her head.

"No, I do not want to tell you."

I assured her that if she told me she would never have this dream again. I promised to never tell anyone. The entire time, my hand was softly rubbing her back as I held her. Eventually, she shared her horrors of being raped. As she painstakingly began to move her lips, tears rolled down her cheeks. She made no effort to wipe them from her face. Her body shook.

"The boys at my school raped me. I was helpless." Her voice became louder. "I cried out and no one heard my desperate cries. I laid there with torn clothes. My body was riddled with pain from where they hit me and kicked me before they violated me. My entire soul ached. No one came to help. Again, and again, I see the boys coming for me. I tried to yell, but my mouth wouldn't open. I tried to run, but my feet wouldn't move."

She placed her head on my shoulder. I softly kissed the back of her neck and our bodies were united as one under the covers. In the morning, that was how they found us: Fiora in her boy's T-shirt and me in my birthday suit. Again, there was no punishment for sleeping in the same bed. The nurse simply suggested that we prepare for morning yoga, and Fiora darted out of the room like a rabbit.

After lunch, I went to my individual therapy session and, again, Hilda was there in place of my usual therapist. In the session, I intentionally failed to mention the previous night's sleep over. I hid my freshly polished nails between my knees as she talked to me.

As the therapy session was ending, Hilda peered over her glasses at me. She said, "Please consider wearing a long shirt and bloomers to bed. Just in case you have visitors in the future."

I agreed to Hilda's request. She seemed to know everything that occurred in the clinic and the Compound, as if there were security cameras in the rooms. She had tested me, to see how forthcoming I would be. She did not need to ask me about last night because she already knew the answers.

Later, I learned that Fiora openly shared with her therapist the details of our friendship. To her, it was a relationship. She talked in her session about the romantic feelings she had for me. Unfortunately, I was clueless. I thought we were just friends and didn't know better.

The following weeks and months we jumped into each other's beds regularly. No reason was necessary. We loved each other's companionship. We were now best friends and we wanted to lie together, tell stories, and giggle. It was the first time I had a true friend, besides Gabrielle. Eventually, we fell asleep, regularly in the same bed without thoughts of getting physical.

Fiora gave me a reason to believe my life was worth living again.

We played dress up. I always wore bottoms, never exposing my private area, partly because I wished that my penis wasn't there. I never considered our games to be anything other than play. I thought that's what girlfriends normally did when they got together. I did not realize how emotionally close our relationship had become.

Hilda closed her eyes to our sleeping arrangements and had a blind eye to our affair of the heart, since our friendship was helping cure our emotional and psychological wounds. My heart, for the first time, felt full again. In our one-on-one session, I told Alicia, "I love every minute I spend with Fiora. It is like heaven. I have never had a best friend before. Oops, I forgot. Gabrielle is my best friend, but you know, that's different."

Alicia was pleased that I was attaining the goals that Hilda set for me. She said, "It is amazing the progress you are making. I hope you realize that you have two wonderful friendships with two individuals who love and care about you. Having supportive, close friends is something rare. Months ago, you were incapable of maintaining these relationships."

I agreed with her.

She said, "These strong friendships will allow you set aside the past and began living for your future. Do

118

you realize how much you have accomplished? You should be very proud of yourself."

I looked at her, gathered my thoughts and realized that I had, indeed, changed. I liked myself and felt more comfortable in who I was. I said, "I cannot ever repay you for all that you have done for me. I am grateful that I have so many people who have helped me on this road to recovery. I believe that living as a woman has made much of this possible."

Alicia nodded. I was completing my third month of having estrogen hormone injections; it had been four months since the bombing. I noticed that my breasts were experiencing sensitivity and my nipples were changing their character. Most of the time it felt painful. I observed that my nipples were budding, and my breasts were enlarging. To my delight, I noticed some slight cleavage.

After my afternoon yoga class, I rinsed off in the facility shower. Fiora moved aside the plastic shower curtain and stuck her head in to tell me something. Suddenly, her eyes widened. From her reaction, she noticed my breasts. She was speechless. I covered my penis with my hand and crossed my legs. I stood there with my breasts exposed. The water dribbled down my body. I did not know how to react, so I didn't. She closed the curtain without saying a word.

That night, she came to my room again. I did not see or hear her enter. My lights were off, and I was curled up in my bed under the sheets. She woke me up, commanding me to sit up in bed and keep quiet. She lifted my jersey shirt over my head. I raised my arms towards the ceiling. When the shirt was off, she wrapped it around my face, as a blindfold.

She took her tongue and gently teased my nipples and breasts. My body was flooded with pleasure. I didn't need to see what was happening to know how good it felt.

The smile on my face expressed a thousand words of emotional pleasure. I was barely able to catch my breath and my heart was pounding. I could not stay still. Fiora removed her shirt and permitted me to kiss her full, beautiful breasts with the same tender care as she touched mine. Then, we dove under the covers, where she instructed me how she wanted me to pleasure her body first with my fingers and then my hand. I felt like an animal devouring its dinner. I benefited from her excitement.

She grunted with pleasure, blushed deeply, then giggled. She requested that I stop and simply hold her. As I hugged her, I asked her why she laughed. She softly shushed me and covered her red face with her hands. I thought back to the B&B in England, when I heard similar noises that Cristina made through the walls. Fiora intentionally tried to control the volume of her voice to keep our sex a secret.

I wished I could experience those sensations she felt. I could only hope that, in time, I would. Fiora was still in my arms when the morning alarm sounded. We had been lovers all along and I was the last to realize it. I had come to the clinic to get healthy; I was not looking for a lover. Until she touched me, I thought I was incapable of having a physical relationship with anyone.

During therapy, I spilled the beans. I had to tell someone, and Alicia was that person. I cried as I shared my heart with Alicia. "Maybe it's the estrogen," I said. "But I love Fiora and I wish this minute that I could be a complete woman so that she could touch my entire body. I want to feel the pleasure that she feels."

Alicia looked at me. My disclosure about a patient-patient relationship had crossed the clinic's red line. She would have to inform Hilda. Maybe I should not have shared such intimate details with Alicia, but I was so happy. I wanted the world to know.

I asked, "Is this how it feels to be in love? I long to be with Fiora constantly. My body craves her. I am euphoric when my skin touches hers."

Alicia smiled warmly. "Yes, that's love."

Hilda came up to me in the hall between classes and asked me to accompany her to her office. She placed her hand tenderly on my shoulder. She said, "I am going to permit the two of you to continue with your relationship, as long as the physical affections remain in your room, after dark. Do we understand each other?"

Nervously, I nodded my agreement.

Hilda said, "Please be careful. In the future, you two may move to different parts of the world. Cherish the time you have together. Remember, people who love you will always love you because of who you are as a person, not because of your gender."

I did not understand why she was giving me this warning. Did she know something that I did not? Was there a hidden message in her comments about love and gender?

With Hilda's consent, Fiora and I went on off-campus dates. We went to the local town for dinners and movies. The Compound's vehicle dropped us off and picked us up at a scheduled time afterwards. On one occasion, Hilda allowed us to spend a weekend shopping and seeing the sights in Paris. The trip to Paris was chaperoned by a staff member who slept in an adjoining room. Our love was growing for each other, becoming more intense and passionate every day. I never wanted to get off the merry-go-round.

Saturday evenings, Gabrielle and I went into town to the local pub. There were times when Gabrielle invited Fiora to join us on our girls' nights out. By doing so, I felt that Gabrielle blessed my relationship with Fiora. Later, I learned that we were always being shadowed by Hilda's spies. Hilda needed to observe how Fiora and I interacted in real life situations. Hilda needed to determine if Fiora could handle co-ed situations without the constant fear of being harmed. Fiora had severe post-traumatic stress that might be triggered in environments where there were men, like in a pub, so our dates were meant to test if we were ready to graduate.

Hilda watched to see how we interacted as women with strangers in unfamiliar surroundings. She observed how we conducted ourselves as lesbian lovers in public places. When the reports came back that we were comfortable, Hilda was pleased. It meant her patients had made significant social progress. Therapy and counseling sessions had prepared us to live outside of the Compound. We were ready to move on.

After months of hormone therapy, my personality and figure became more notably feminine. I was surprised how much I had changed. I drew closer to Fiora, as well. I was sure that I wanted to spend the rest of my life with her.

One night, we lay in bed with my head on her shoulder, my right leg positioned between her legs, and my thigh touching her pelvis. It was our usual position as we started our pillow talk. I thought to myself, *Damn these hormones.* I was finding myself in tears when I grabbed her tightly and said, "I never want to leave you. I want us to be together forever."

She laughed. "You silly girl, we have a lifetime to live together after college. First, you need time for your sexual replacement surgery and to earn a degree. I too need to finish school. We will always be lovers and there will be plenty of time for us."

With trepidation, I asked, "Are you planning to leave anytime soon? Have you applied to college?"

She said, "I received information from a college's accredited nursing program last week. I was afraid to discuss it with you until I knew more. Forgive me, I am sorry. I have a college interview in two weeks in Tel Aviv. My cousin lives there, and I will be able to share an apartment with her. If I like the school, I will probably go there. My cousin and I were close when I lived outside Paris. She is five years older and said she would assist me with the language and the culture."

"Why did you choose Tel Aviv?"

She explained, "Hilda helped me in my selection process."

I thought to myself that I should have seen Hilda's fingerprints all over this.

Fiora said, "The city of Tel Aviv is very accepting of gays and lesbians. Hilda felt that it was a big plus that I have family there. It is a great school for nursing."

With a smile, I said, "You're Jewish? My mother would be so happy to know that I am dating a Jewish girl."

"I do not think your mother would recognize you in this pink lace bra."

We both laughed until we fell asleep. I closed my eyes wondering what my future would be like without her.

Chapter 18

As hormone therapy continued, I noticed more changes to my body. My skin softened. My body hair was thinning and became shinier and easier to shave. In many places, body hair stopped growing. I underwent a series of laser treatments to permanently eliminate facial and body hair. The hair on my head grew past my shoulders, so I learned to put it up with a hair clip.

The hormones affected my emotions and my weight. Initially, my mood swings resembled a roller coaster. I learned to live with the mood changes, although I was prone to crying more often than I had prior to starting estrogen. To combat the weight gain, I simply decreased my caloric intake and ran three miles every day.

I noticed a redistribution of my body weight to my thighs and butt. They were now shapely and feminine. When I wore jeans to town or at the pub, young men turned their heads to check me out.

John and Charles graduated. They planned to be roommates in London. I had been thinking about my future, too. I applied to the University of Cambridge's College of Computer Science. It had classes in gaming software design. More importantly, I desired to be close to Gabrielle when she returned to London. She was the combination of another figure and best friend, that I needed in my life.

I also considered the timing of my sexual reassignment surgery. I had lots of questions that needed to be answered. There was preparation and recovery time that must be factored in. I could not expect to start classes before I recovered from the surgery. To play it safe, I reapplied to Northwestern University McCormick School of Engineering, in Evanston, Illinois. Northwestern was still my dream.

I regularly called or sent text messages to Jack to keep up our relationship and with the news on the home front. Helen, Jack's wife, was still not doing well. From our conversations, it was apparent that Jack was depressed because of Helen's deteriorating health.

When he called to check in, his voice was glum. "I'm sorry for calling so early in the morning, but would you consider coming home for Passover? It starts the first week of April. It might be the last one with Helen in attendance I'm afraid to say. It would mean a lot to all of us if you were here."

I realized what he meant, and my tone was somber when I answered him. "Don't talk like that. They'll find a cure. Yes, of course, I will be there for Passover. Would it be okay if I bring a friend with me?"

"Of course. Bring Gabrielle. How thoughtless of me not to include her."

"I'll make plans to arrive a day or two before the holiday begins, so I can assist with the preparations. Thank you for including me as part of the family. It means more than I can express in words."

I had hoped to ask Fiora and Gabrielle to join me, but I knew from an earlier conversation that Fiora would be in Israel. She had come running up to me that morning with a piece of paper in her outstretched hand. "I'm in! I finally received my acceptance from Tel Aviv School of Nursing."

I hugged her and jumped for joy with her. I did so partly because I was happy for her and partly because she was so excited. I did not want to spoil her elation. My voice quivered as I asked, "So, Fiora, when does the school year start? How much time will we have before you must leave me?"

"The program starts in the fall, but they want me to report this week for the start of the Ulpan program. It's a crash course in the Hebrew language." With regret in her voice, she added, "I must leave in the next couple of days, but we will always be connected. You are just a text or phone call away. You are my first and only love. Maybe after your surgeries, you could study in Israel? Close to me!"

Fiora left the Compound and again my bed was cold. I was the last one from my group still here. Truthfully, I was depressed and, when others were not around, I cried. I sent Fiora a text message: 'Good luck, love always!' I wanted to run after her, but knew I had to first complete what I started. I would go back to Ohio for Passover and have faith that, if it was meant to be, Fiora would stay in my life.

Gabrielle knew I was in bad way. She tried to console me that week. After Fiora left, Gabrielle came into my room with a sense of urgency. "Girl, put on your clothes. We are going to town tonight. I could use a drink."

I could always count on Gabrielle to cheer me up and lift my spirits. I wiped tears from my eyes, put on a happy face, and slid on a pair of body-hugging black jeans.

Gabrielle smiled. "Forget the make-up. Just put on a sweater. You are going out with your big sister."

Chapter 19

Gabrielle and I drove down the dark single lane road to the local town. I listened to the call of the winter wind against the car's windows. The roads had been freshly plowed but were still dangerous. This was the only road to the local pub, which served hot and cold food and a variety of alcoholic beverages. It was the only place for miles to go for evening entertainment. Both young and old, came to here to socialize with friends and neighbors. Some brought their dates.

We walked through two sets of doors. The outer doors kept the cold wind out. The inner doors served as the entrance to the pub. Gabrielle and I had been regulars here every Saturday night for the last month. I viewed the familiar, three-room smoke-filled establishment seeking a vacant table. On the way to the table, we greeted local acquaintances.

We shook off the cold and ice, and removed our hats and scarves, but kept our unbuttoned coats on for a while, until we warmed up. We wore warm, water-resistant rabbit fur-lined brown boots that laced in the front. We dressed like sisters, nearly matching and definitely coordinated. I wore a flattering, light blue sweater and Gabrielle wore a bulky brown wool Vneck. I was relieved to be out of the Compound and at a place where I could relax and blow off steam.

We listened to the piped-in rock songs from the 1960s and 1970s, which played from the ceiling through mounted speakers. We joked about how mild the winter had been until the last couple of weeks. Tonight, the northern winds were simply brutal. A barmaid came to take our order. I requested a glass of Malbec. Gabrielle asked for a light beer on tap. Cheese curds and a couple of Bavarian pretzels rounded off our appetizers.

In moments, the beer arrived with a piece of orange fruit dangling on the rim of the ice-cold mug. I picked up my glass of Malbec wine and said, "Tonight, I am going to enjoy myself. Screw the diet. If I get 'pissed', to use your term, then I hope you can carry me to the car. I am going to eat and drink as much as I want, and I won't feel guilty until the morning."

Gabrielle's eyes sparkled as she said, "That's my girl! I am glad you are going to join the living again. You are going to have many more lovers. Just remember, we will always have each other."

We touched our glasses together before drinking. The second round soon followed. We made some stupid toasts. We looked around the pub, compared notes and determined that there were just a couple of cute, available young girls and guys. While Gabrielle glanced at both, I only eyed the young women.

Gabrielle said, "I am planning to give notice to Hilda next week and move back to London. I hope you will join me and be my roommate? After seven months of hard labor and Hilda's demanding schedule, I need a vacation to relax. A place where we can eat, drink and be merry. What are your thoughts? Do you have any suggestions about where we should go?"

With excitement, I didn't hesitate to say, "I'm dying for a vacation too. However, I don't want to veg; I want an adventure. May I offer you my idea?"

Gabrielle smiled and nodded her head.

My eyes widened with excitement as I shared my thoughts. "Have you ever gone skiing? Ever since I saw a James Bond movie filmed in Switzerland, I have wanted to travel there and stay at a spa. I would love to hit the slopes and sit in a hot tub drinking a flute of champagne." My voice became more excited. "In the movies and magazines, the slopes look so glamorous. If that is something you would like to do, let me treat you and pay for the getaway. It's the least I can do to show you my gratitude for everything you have done for me."

Gabrielle tipped her glass in my direction. It was a deal.

I continued. "On a sad note, Jack called this morning. His wife is definitely dying. The family wants me to participate in her last Passover in Cleveland. The Jewish holiday starts the first week of April. Please come with me. I am scared to go back to Cleveland alone. I am afraid of being around people who knew me as Marc. I need your emotional support. Can you be there with me, to give me strength? We would be there for four days at most, and then we would have two weeks to travel and visit several cities and tourist sights. Please say yes!"

At first, Gabrielle was quiet as she digested my words. Then, she grinned. "Gosh, I do not know where to start. What do I say? I would love to tour the States. I have never skied. It would be fun to learn, but I don't have the clothes or the equipment for skiing."

"No problem. We can take lessons and have fun shopping for clothes. We can rent equipment from the chalet. I have heard that there are lots of cute, single guys who ski. Who knows, maybe you'll get lucky."

We both laughed and got excited thinking of the trip. Then I got serious. "Gabrielle, how many people can say that their sister is also their closest friend? Thank you for everything."

Gabrielle smiled. She said, "Back at you. I am grateful for the times I needed your emotional support. I value our friendship; you are my best friend."

Gabrielle put her hand on my back and continued. She said, "I hope you realize how much you have accomplished this past seven months. When you arrived at the Compound, you spoke in one-word sentences and failed to maintain eye contact with people. Initially, you avoided help from Alicia, Hilda, and anyone else for that matter. Yet, you've changed. I can tell by the way you handled Fiora's departure. You are an incredible woman."

We hugged. I cried, but then pulled myself together. Even through my tears, I had a smile on my face.

Gabrielle said, "Are you sure you want me to join you in the States? Don't you want to be alone with Jack and his family?"

"We will have an awesome time together."

Her eyes glittered. "I always wanted to cross the pond, but between relationships and work, I never made the time to go. This is a dream come true."

I tried to change the subject, but Gabrielle wouldn't bite. She shook her head and said, "Not to dampen our plans, but we need to discuss your surgery options. You have choices. You do not have to go through with reassignment surgery; you can stay the way you are. The surgery is painful and permanent. However, if you decide to have surgery you should schedule it for a week after we return from our travels. That way you could recuperate before starting college."

We cut our conversation short when two young hunks in their twenties came up to our table. They were wearing leather work boots and T-shirts under long-sleeved plaid work shirts. The shirts were not tucked into their distressed looking jeans. They may not have been the most intelligent men, but they possessed other physical qualities. They were cute and had incredible muscular bodies. I could tell from their accents that they were Eastern European migrant workers.

The guys grabbed two empty chairs and invited themselves to our table. I thought I would be doing Gabrielle a favor by encouraging them. They asked if we spoke German or Russian. We told them that we only spoke English and Gabrielle advised them to keep on moving. The pub was hopping and noisy and we had to sit close to hear one another.

"Where are you from?" I asked. If I was smart, I would have told them to find another table, but I liked the idea that the two hunks thought we were two hot-looking women.

The taller one, who spoke better broken English, said, "Why you nice women here?"

With a sharp tongue, Gabrielle told them to shove off. She said, "We are here for drinks and to have a private conversation, so bugger off."

Her index finger pointed to the exit sign. In the UK, a gent would have taken the first hint and bid us a good evening. These two were no gentlemen. They just grinned at each other. Since they were staying, I decided to have fun with them and test my femininity. Annoyed, Gabrielle kicked me twice under the table.

She wanted me to ignore them. I wanted to engage in harmless flirting. "So, what kind of work do you do?" I asked.

In a heavy accent, the taller of the two said, "We are construction workers. Now, we work on roads, moving away snow." He used his hands to illustrate how the plow worked.

I said, "You must be very strong to do that kind of work."

He made a muscle, flexing his right arm.

"With your shirt on, I can't see anything," I said in a high-pitched giggling voice. I put my hands on my cheeks. Gabrielle rolled her eyes and shook her head. I continued, "Can we can see your muscles?"

Almost immediately, they stripped their shirts off and the taller one flexed his right arm and made a muscle. I leaned over to him and placed both of my hands on his bicep. Again, in the same stupid voice, I said, "Oh, look how big your muscle is. Look, Gabrielle."

She turned beet red and slid down like she wanted to hide under the table. The bouncers observed these two bare chested blokes and immediately came to our table. "Either put your shirts on and obey the rules or leave."

They complied immediately, picking their shirts off the wet floor. After downing a drink, they asked us to join them elsewhere. Gabrielle realized that they meant the backseat of a work truck. They wanted one thing and it was not casual conversation. Let's face it, I didn't understand half the words they were saying. Gabrielle's sour mood was catching, and I was not sure how much they wanted to understand when she said, "Sod off."

I looked to the bigger guy and said, "I cannot have sex. I have decided to become a nun. I am taking the vow of chastity next week."

Noting he had difficulty with the language, I explained it to him in French: "I am a virgin and I will become a nun next week."

The two of them had blank stares on their faces. Gabrielle squirmed in her chair and tried to keep a straight face. She bit her lip so she would not laugh out loud.

The taller guy questioned Gabrielle, "You want her nun?"

"Yes, I think she would be a wonderful nun. Our mother does not want her to be a nun."

"Listen to mama. No be nun, nuns ugly. Come to truck. We go boom-boom and you never want to be nun again." He wiggled his eyebrows at me.

I said, "Sorry, we have to go home now, otherwise our mother will worry."

As I tried to stand, the closer one to me grabbed my arm and pulled me down. I was nervously sweating. What did I start? This could be a real firestorm. I looked around, considering an exit strategy. I was ready to stand on my chair and yell for help, hoping that the bouncers would hear my voice above the music. From the corner of my eye, I saw the cavalry stomping toward our table in the person of Hilda branding a red, unhappy face.

She approached the table, yelling in a loud, blistering voice, "What are you girls doing?"

I looked to the guys and announced, "This is our mother."

Hilda said sharply, "Boys, it is time for you to go home."

The taller one pulled his friend's sleeve as if to say, *forget it.*

As they walked away, the other guy looked at Hilda and pleaded, "Do not let her do it."

"Okay, girls. Will you please tell me what was happening here?" Hilda sat down at the table, wearing the look of disappointment, like a mother who knew that her children had misbehaved, and she wanted answers — now!

Gabrielle started. "It's my fault. I know better than to be talking to these kinds of guys."

I interrupted. Words flew out of my mouth at a record setting pace. "It's my fault. I thought that I could string them along and I did not know how to stop them once things got heated. I told them that I was going to be a nun and take a vow of chastity. They wanted to be virgin slayers and save me from a fate worse than death."

Hilda laughed hysterically. "You two are definitely torn from the same cloth. What will I do with you two?"

Hilda turned to Gabrielle as I left the table to get another round. I overheard her say to Gabrielle, "She reminds me of you. She needs to learn about men before she gets in trouble."

When I came back, Gabrielle asked Hilda, "How did you know where we were? How did you know we were in trouble?"

Hilda smiled, "I have my spies."

Gabrielle and I looked around the room but didn't recognize a soul. The three of us socialized and drank for another hour, before Hilda left. When we were alone, I apologized to Gabrielle. I told her that I thought I would enjoy the attention of two men who said we were hot girls. She hit me in the arm. Then, she scolded me.

"Dearie, to a horny bloke, every woman looks enticing and attractive. The more they drink, the prettier we look and the more they will want us. They think with their tallywackers," she said.

It grew late. Gabrielle and I got back in the car and started up the road, heading back to the Compound. It was lonely and dark. The only light came from an occasional passing car. From the beam of our headlights and the quick pace of wiper blades going back and forth, the snowfall was hypnotizing.

Gabrielle continued our earlier conversation. She said, "Are you considering not having the surgery?"

"First, tell me how the procedure was for you," I said.

Gabrielle looked stunned. She took her eyes off the road and stared at me. She pulled the vehicle into a closed petrol station.

"How did you know?"

"When we first met, you told me that you were born unable to have children. You said you didn't have the right plumbing. If you had a uterus, you probably could

138

still have a child with someone else's fertilized egg. Then, tonight, Hilda said that we were two of a kind. Also, why would you have come to the Compound had you not experienced sexual trauma issues? I put it together."

Gabrielle's expression and her tone were resolute. "Ms Sherlock Holmes, you are correct, but that is *my* secret. The only time I trusted someone with this knowledge, he betrayed me. He could not handle that I was born with a boy's body. There is a lesson for you. Never tell your future lovers or friends your secret. Men, and even some women, cannot handle the truth. They are afraid of public perceptions. You will find some people can be unforgiving and unaccepting of your choices."

I nodded. I understood she was telling the truth as she experienced it.

Gabrielle's tone softened. "You will need three months to recover from the reconstructive operation. Then, you will need someone to take care of you for at least three weeks on a regular basis after the surgery. Depression after the procedure is normal. I will be there for you." I was overwhelmed by her offer to be both my therapist and caregiver, too.

Gabrielle took a deep breath. "The best timing for surgery would be within a week after our return from the States. You would have ample time to recuperate before the start of your classes and I am able to delay my return to work by three months. How does that work for you?"

"Are you glad you had the surgery? Would you have done it any differently?"

She blushed. "I'm not trying to push you one way or the other. You do not have to have the surgery. You can live a fruitful life without the SRS. I am not you. I am happy with my life decision."

"I am ready to complete my evolution as a woman. When we get back, I'll schedule the date. By the way, your secret is safe with me, always."

Gabrielle's urgent tone returned. "Marci, about this evening. As a girl, men will want to physically take advantage of you. If a guy drinks too much, he believes that he has the God-given right to have sex. If you get drunk, men will take advantage of you. As you saw tonight, they wouldn't take 'no' for an answer. Just being in a room alone with a guy can also be dangerous. They have the strength to overpower us. Understand? Enough said?"

"Yes, Mom, I will try to be more careful in the future," I joked, though I knew she was dead serious.

"Very cute," Gabrielle said. "So, tell me, how are you planning on returning to the States?"

"What do you mean? I have a United States passport and I will board the plane."

"Whose name is on the passport?"

"Oh, shit. It's Marc's passport," I said. "What do I do? I am no longer Marc."

"When we get back to London, you will need to visit the US embassy and apply for a new, expedited passport. You will need to bring your EEA travel documents and a letter from Hilda explaining that you have changed genders and are under her professional care."

"I guess I will be busy once we return to London."

Chapter 20

We rode the train to Paris and then the high-speed Eurostar from Paris to London. From there, we took a taxi to Gabrielle's flat. We discussed and dreamed about our Switzerland vacation, the sights we would see, and the clothes we would buy. We planned to refresh our wardrobe for our US visit. Our joyful feelings of anticipation left us in a state of euphoria as we giggled and laughed during our travels.

When we got close to Gabrielle's building, her mood shifted. As we approached the entrance to the flat, Gabrielle hesitated. Her apprehension was obvious as she stared at the door. I waited, and then realized why she was crying.

I took the key from her hand, unlocked the door, and hugged her. I whispered, "You know Cristina wanted you to live and be happy."

Without another word, Gabrielle took a few wobbly steps over the threshold into the flat. As soon as she saw the framed pictures of herself and Cristina smiling and holding hands, she dropped her luggage. The whole apartment was a shrine to their relationship and, therefore, the ghosts remained.

Gabrielle could not help herself. She sobbed helplessly. I led her to the master bedroom.

We laid on the bed and I held her without a word being said. After several minutes, I whispered, "We must leave. I need to take care of my passport and we have errands to run before our flight. Let's get going. You would tell me that we must live for today not yesterday. Right?"

She nodded her head, got up, and opened the windows to air out the flat. We taxied to the Snow+Rock store. There, we found beautifully designed, colorful ski pants with matching jackets, ski gloves, hats and scarves. I hoped the shopping experience would re-energize Gabrielle. It didn't. She was clearly coping with deep emotions and couldn't focus on the moment.

When outerwear failed to cheer her up, I suggested we shop for sexy intimate apparel. With a perky voice, I said, "We need to go back to the Harvey Nichols department store to bolster our limited wardrobes."

On the walk, I grabbed her arm. "Listen, in several days we will be on the slopes, just you and me. Think about the beautiful scenery and the beautiful men. Think of how we will shine in our new outfits."

The clothes at Nichols were amazing, colorful, beautiful and sexy. I got so carried away, Gabrielle had to take my charge card away from me. My ever-changing body needed an updated wardrobe to conform to my feminine figure. My old bras were uncomfortably small and I didn't own any sexy nightwear.

Since I was going all-out at the lingerie counter, I picked a variety of bras, one to wear with each outfit. As I struggled in the fitting room, I realized how clueless guys are about beauty. They had no comprehension how complicated women's clothes and accessories are, or what women must do every day to maintain our look.

We left the store and headed to the US embassy. We entered its protective gates, guided by the armed guard to the passport office. When it was my turn to be assisted, I stepped forward to the passport desk. A handsome young man was ready to assist me. He looked me over with a devilish smile. I knew what was on his mind.

"How may I support you today?" he asked.

With a friendly smile, I told him. "I am returning to the States in five days and I realized that I need to change the name on my passport before I leave."

"Recently married or divorced?" His eyes sparkled as he emphasized the word *divorced*.

Quietly, so others in the lobby queue would not overhear me, I said, "No. The passport reflects my previous gender and my former name."

I held my breath, waiting for his response. His interest deflated immediately. His intentions became strictly professional and administrative. I handed over my passport, driver's license, the physician's letter from

Hilda, and a European Union travel document under my new name. The clerk informed me that my passport would be waiting for me in plenty of time before my departure date to the States. In a neutral, non-flirtatious tone, he wished me a safe journey and called for the next person in line.

I was relieved. I had feared that this experience at the embassy would be confrontational. I found I could breathe again.

We returned to the flat. Gabrielle remained unwilling to discuss her feelings. She maintained that damn British stiff upper lip and pretended that her sadness was under control. I hoped this trip would help repair her soul.

We packed for a four-day stay at the St Moritz Club Med. We planned to attend yoga and ski classes. In the evenings we planned to go club hopping. I was planning to party, enjoy my freedom from the Compound, as I kicked off a new chapter in my life.

On the flight from London to Zurich, Gabrielle barely spoke a single word. On the train to St Moritz, she stared aimlessly out of the window. I am sure she didn't notice the beautiful snow-capped mountains or the snow glimmering in the sun's rays. She remained an emotionless zombie.

After hours of travel, we arrived at St Moritz. We walked around the centuries-old European town while waiting for our transport. The stores were very stylish, for this was the playground of the rich.

From St Moritz, we boarded the transport to the Club Med Roi Soleil resort. This was an inclusive resort, so all the food, alcohol, exercise classes, ski lessons, lift tickets and other amenities were included in the price of our vacation. However, we did tip the valet who brought us up to our room.

We had booked a simple room, with two queen-sized beds, a walnut wood dresser, a small closet, and a flat screen television. I did not care for the decor, but it didn't matter, since we were planning to spend much of the time on the slopes and night clubs.

We unpacked and had an early dinner at a casual restaurant before we confirmed our schedules for our stay with the front desk. We signed up for yoga classes and ski lessons and made dinner reservations. The desk clerk recommended we book our fine dining reservation at the preferred restaurants in advance because of limited daily availability.

After dinner our first night, we sat at the bar, drank wine, and listened to music. We turned in early to prepare for the next day's intense schedule of morning classes, skiing and late evening entertainment.

Morning arrived too soon. Regardless, at seven a.m., we attended a yoga class. We looked like sisters in our matching outfits: black leggings with bright yellow piping on the sides, with matching black sports bras. I covered up more than Gabrielle, with a gray yoga crop tank top.

I hoped the yoga class stretching would prepare our bodies for skiing. Afterwards, we showered and dressed for the slopes. We walked outside to the ski instructor's hut looking for Kristi, our instructor. She greeted us with a smile and promised us a day of fun. For three hours, she taught us the basics and had us going downhill on easier, less challenging slopes. In March, the weather was warmer, but still cold enough to keep the slopes intact.

After skiing, we returned to the room to recuperate and munch before returning to the slopes for another two hours of skiing. As I glided down the hills, cold snowflakes gently smacked my face as my skis cut into the soft snow. It was a dream come true, and the thrill of a lifetime.

Of course, I fell on my butt more than once. My thighs were sore from crouching down on the skis. The more I fell, the more Gabrielle laughed. When she wiped out, I laughed at her. Absorbing the beauty of the mountains and the cold, clean air was a priceless life experience. Today's activities revived Gabrielle's spirits.

We changed into our swimsuits and soaked in the hot tub. The mineral waters temporarily melted our aches and pains as they circulated around us. While sitting in the tub, we sipped cold, alcoholic, sweet beverages, just like in the movies. Afterwards we showered and then napped before dressing for a late night at the clubs.

Our slinky, backless, mini dresses barely covered our derrieres. We had reservations at the Corviglia restaurant, Club Med's upscale dining facility. We started with several glasses of wine and appetizers. I chose salmon and Gabrielle had the medium rare steak as our main courses. For dessert we drank port wine and shared a chocolate mousse.

We tottered into the nightclub. I saw a delicious-looking drink at the next table, so I asked the waitress the name of it and ordered one. It was a Long Island Iced Tea, with an orange and cherry garnish. Gabrielle ordered another glass of red wine.

"Be careful, you are drinking a serious cocktail," Gabrielle warned. I sipped the drink and could not detect any alcohol.

Gabrielle grabbed my hand and said, "I want to teach you how to dance."

It seemed like every other girl around me was capable of dancing. Gabrielle pulled me across the dance floor and guided my body with her hands as I tried to feel the flow of the music. I could not coordinate my movements and felt totally frustrated.

Gabrielle teased, "You are a lost cause. But don't worry, I will still dance with you."

I told her that I needed a break. I went back to our table, finished my first drink, and then started on a second one. If there were more after that, I don't remember. After my second drink, I got up and told Gabrielle that I would give it another try.

The alcohol didn't help. Finally, I gave up. I said, "I am sorry, but I am a total failure. Go have fun and I'll watch."

As I left the floor, our ski instructor, Kristi, came up to Gabrielle. They exchanged several words and then began dancing together. Well, that's all I remembered until the morning.

When I looked up from my pillow with a hangover headache, I thought I was seeing double; Kristi and Gabrielle were fast asleep in the other bed. I brushed my teeth and showered. By the time I opened the bathroom door only Gabrielle was left in the bed.

She sat up and rubbed her eyes. "Marci, I am sorry, I guess I…"

"No explanation is necessary. We are not children. I just hope you had a good time."

She smiled. That grin of hers said everything that needed to be said. I guess the ghosts had disappeared. After that affair, Gabrielle was ready to enjoy the rest of our trip.

This morning neither of us were in condition to tackle the slopes or attend yoga classes. My calf muscles were sore, my legs ached and, to quote the Scottish, I had a wee bit of a hangover. I convinced Gabrielle that we should have breakfast and indulge ourselves in deep tissue massages.

Unfortunately, the earliest available massage appointments were not until the afternoon. So, with time to kill, we sat in a comfortable loveseat facing the large bay windows on the first floor of the lodge. We had warm lattes and scones as we took in the scenery of mountain ranges filled with countless skiers. We leaned back and chatted.

"So, what do you want to do tonight?" Gabrielle asked.

"I was hoping for a nice quiet dinner, with a little less alcohol. Then, let's play it by ear. Is that okay with you?"

"In the meantime, I have questions and would appreciate your perspective. It is not my intension to make you uncomfortable, but I need to know why you agreed to have the surgery. It will help me in my decision-making process."

Gabrielle's feet were propped on the coffee table, a latte held in both hands, and her face was serene. As I asked, I saw the tension rise in her face. She placed her feet on the ground. Her eyes stared at the cup and then at me. In spite of her obvious anxiety, she cleared her throat and made light of my question. "You want to play twenty questions? Let's do it."

I started with the biggest question of all. "How did you know that you wanted to be a girl?"

"I have never discussed this with anyone, except for Hilda. These are my sacred feelings and you must promise never to violate my trust. Never tell another soul, understand? Do I have your solemn promise?"

I nodded my head, which she understood as my acceptance of her condition. I could hardly wait. She was finally going to share her inner secret with me. I hoped I wasn't opening a Pandora's box of trauma that would ruin our friendship.

She took a deep breath before she began. "I had been physically abused by my father for many years. I started to dress as a girl as a defense mechanism so that my father would leave me alone. Maybe I pretended to be someone else so that what was happening was being inflicted on that 'someone else' and not me. I became a different person and lived as 'her'. My brain told me that if I was a girl, my father would not be doing bad things to *me*."

With watery eyes she continued. "My Dad was hurting Gabrielle and not me. After a while, the previous 'me' ceased to exist and only 'Gabrielle' remained. At that point, I wanted to remain a girl. That year, the doctors medically approved hormone replacement. I believe that my gender identity started as a result of childhood trauma."

She took a sip of coffee holding the mug with two hands as she drew up the courage to continue. "A therapist at the secondary school I attended sat me down and asked me questions about why I wanted to be a girl and why I was a loner. At the time, I was sixteen. I did not want to socialize with my peers because I was afraid that they would learn my secret. Obviously, I did not know back then what I know now."

"I blurted to the school therapist, the truth, that my father inappropriately touched me at night. And I begged her not to tell him as he would hurt me. The therapist had seen bruises and heard similar stories like this before. She called the police and my father was questioned and then arrested. That was the last time I saw him. The doctors sent me to the Compound for psychological therapy. I later learned my father was sentenced to prison where he died shortly after he arrived."

"I'm so sorry," I said as I comfortingly placed my hand on hers. "Are you sure you want to continue?"

"Years ago, doctors did not know what we know now as to the effects of hormones. We have data that indicates that teenagers change their minds when it comes to their gender. Many prefer their assigned gender, but how many of them are encouraged to explore it, without terrible social consequences? Transgender and gay children have a high suicide rate and are ostracized at home and school. They are the most likely to become homeless when their families reject them."

"I was pre-puberty when I started on the hormones a year before I arrived at Hilda's. I had the body of a young female with developing breasts. Mentally, I was a basket case scared of my own shadow."

Gabrielle took another sip and said, "I was to stay with Hilda for a year. Hilda took pity on me and spent countless hours counseling me. During that year, my breasts continued to develop, along with my feminine facial and physical characteristics."

"Hilda was there to hold me and love me. When the year was over, she would not let me return home. She convinced my mother that I should remain and work at the clinic and pursue a nursing degree. I'm glad she did. Hilda supported my decision to have surgery and was there for me afterwards like I will be for you. If not for her, I do not know if I would have survived. I will love Hilda until the day I die. I owe her so much."

I absorbed what she had shared with me. Her story wrenched my gut. After a couple minutes of silence, I said, "But, you have dated men. Weren't you afraid that these men would hurt you, too?"

She lowered her head. "I need alcohol but will settle for another latte and a bathroom break before we go any further, okay?"

"I will order you a latte and I'll wait here for you. Are you sure you want to keep talking about this? I'll understand if you want to stop?" I was moved by her confession.

Gabrielle shook her head and said, "Little sister, I am emotionally drained, but I want to continue. It is my hope that you will learn from my experiences." Slowly and deliberately, she walked away from me and didn't return for five minutes.

"Now, where were we? I remember."

Picking up her replaced latte, Gabrielle continued. "Honestly, men scare me. Years of therapy have taught me that I dated older men *because* I wanted the love I never received from my father. Harold was the first man

I really dated. We met at the hospital. He swept me off my feet and was my first lover."

"He was fifteen years older than me. He offered me love. He did not want children because he already had children from his first marriage. He wanted a companion, a lover, and someone to handle the domestic details of his life. After a year of preparation, I was ready to convert to his religion. I had become everything he wanted in a wife."

Gabrielle paused for a second. She looked exhausted but continued. "I did not know what a healthy marriage or relationship looked like and was content having his love and affection. I suspected that he had been unfaithful during our two years together but hoped that marriage would change that. A month before the wedding, I learned he was having an affair with a friend of mine, another nurse. I confronted him and told him I knew about his womanizing."

I covered my mouth with my hand as Gabrielle continued. "I decided to come clean and I told him that I had had gender reconstructive surgery. I had feared him learning the truth later. I threw all the cards on the table so there would be no more secrets between us. Having been lovers for two years, he never had a complaint about my body or the sex. So, I assumed it wouldn't make a difference. I was the same person he'd fallen in love with. I was wrong. The bastard!"

"Did you ever tell Cristina about it?"

"Never! After Harold, I decided that I would never trust anyone again with this secret. I was too afraid to tell Cristina because I didn't know what her reaction would be. Cristina and I loved each other without question. We were best friends. Now that she's gone, I believe she would have understood, and it wouldn't have been an issue. I was looking forward to raising our children together. Our relationship was a dream come true for me. We made each other laugh. That was something that I did not have with any other lover."

I was speechless as she confessed the past. I said, "She was one in a million. I will always miss her." My voice seemed to bring Gabrielle back to earth.

"Let's quit for now," she said. "All this talking has made me hungry. Let's get lunch before our massages, facials and pedicures. Tonight, maybe we'll grab fondue at the Stubi restaurant? By the way, little sister, I am going to monitor your drinking tonight. No mixed drinks for you! You may have two glasses of wine and then I am cutting you off."

Chapter 21

Back in London, after our short but relaxing Switzerland vacation, Gabrielle had an awakening. We re-entered the flat and, this time, she walked straight in and wasn't haunted by Cristina's ghost.

While Gabrielle showered, I went around the various rooms and collected the sentimental birthday cards, anniversary cards and friendship cards that were on display. I also gathered most, but not all of the photographs of Gabrielle and Cristina together. I placed everything on a bedroom closet shelf, out of sight.

After her shower, Gabrielle came back to the living room and noticed the missing mementos. She hugged me with a somber smile, and we went to sleep.

In the morning, like every other day, I took two milligrams of estrogen. In spite of the stress and dramatic changes I'd been through, the realization dawned that the past few months had been my happiest days ever. I was comfortable with who I had become.

When I peered at myself in the mirror, I noticed the same female hormonal outbreaks and teenage insecurities as anyone else my age. I was self-conscious about my weight and appearance like most teenage girls. With anticipation, I looked forward to the surgery, so I could complete my metamorphosis into womanhood, although I still had reservations.

I gazed out at the Thames and wondered if London was my home, now and forever.

We ran over to the US embassy to pick up my new passport, packed our luggage, and enjoyed dinner in Chinatown. The next morning, we headed to Heathrow and boarded a British Airways flight to New York City. We planned two days of sightseeing in The Big Apple before taking our connecting flight to see Jack and Helen.

On the flight to New York, I leaned over to Gabrielle and discreetly asked, "Did you enjoy the sex with Harold? Was it what you expected it to be like?" I'd lost my virginity already, and I'd been with Fiora, but I still hadn't slept with a man as a woman.

Gabrielle was obviously uncomfortable discussing the subject on an airplane full of strangers. She elbowed me and gave me her signature bug-eyed stare. She lowered her chin as she puckered her lips, just like my mother used to when she was angry with me. She maintained that stare for a moment without saying a word. I got the hint. This conversation would be better suited to a later time.

Gabrielle had never been to New York, as she had never ventured across the pond. I had visited it with my Dad to watch a baseball game at Yankee Stadium. If I thought the traffic in London was terrible, it was much worse in the Manhattan borough of New York City. You could literally get out of the cab, sit down and eat a corned beef sandwich at Katz's delicatessen and the traffic would not have moved. We attended a theatrical performance, two dinners, and a stop at the Brighton Store.

If you have never gone to a Brighton Store, you are truly missing a wonderful experience. Gabrielle saw a candy apple red, vintage leather purse in the store window. It called out to her, "You need to buy me!" So, she handed over her credit card in record time. Before I knew it, I had a fuchsia, crossbody bag in my hand and I was waiting for the clerk to process my charge card. I remembered my mother saying, "A girl can never have too many purses." Who was I to argue with Mom?

In the hotel room, before we turned out the lights, I crawled into Gabrielle's queen-sized bed and asked her, "Please tell me what sex was like with Harold. I want to know what sex will be like after the operation."

Gabrielle shook her head at me and said, "Never have I met anyone who asks more questions than you. Let's back up. The surgery is *major* surgery. For weeks afterwards, you will be in pain and that pain will be intense. Your newly-created vagina will need to be dilated three to five times a day."

With a deer-in-the-headlights stare, I asked, "Gabrielle, what does 'dilate' mean?"

"You have pierced ears. Remember how I told you that if you do not continuously wear earrings or studs, eventually the holes will close up and you will need another piercing?"

"Yes, I remember you telling me that."

"Your new vagina will close up unless you insert something into it on a regular basis. The dilation process will keep the vagina from closing by placing hard, plastic dildos into it. They are called dilators. I call them dildos. You will need to keep them inside you for twenty minutes per session. After surgery you will be given four of these dildos to use; each is a different size. You will need to work your way up to the thickest. You will do this from three to five times a day for the first three months."

"Are you serious?" I gasped.

Gabrielle said, "You wanted to know, so I'm telling you. Your vagina will be sore from the surgery. The dilation will be painful, and it will initially be messy. But dilation is something that you must do every day. I had pain performing dilation for the first couple of months after surgery, until my body became accustomed to the thickest dilator."

"But it was better after that, right?"

She nodded. "Putting a dildo inside your body is nothing like a human being thrusting themselves into you. I was terrified the first time I had sex with a man for that exact reason. I was afraid of another person being inside of me. I feared the pain I would experience. But in the end, I wanted to please this man, so I did it. I wanted him to love me forever. I asked another transgender girlfriend for some advice and she instructed me to insert a small amount of lubricant in my vagina to enhance the experience and lessen the pain. Then, I was told that I needed to ride him, cowgirl style, until my vagina was comfortable with intercourse."

"Did you enjoy it?"

"God, no. It hurt the first few times and my body needed a whole month to adjust to his girth and the force of his thrusts. After a lot of practice, it became very enjoyable." Her index finger pointed towards my bed. "No more questions. Go back to your own bed and sleep. I love you and I will see you in the morning."

I kissed her on her cheek and wished her goodnight.

We were to arrive in Cleveland three days before the beginning of the Passover holiday. As time grew near, I confided to Gabrielle that I was afraid to see Jack's children and others who knew me as Marc. "What should I say and how should I act when they see me? I am stressed out of my mind right now. If not for Helen, I would bypass Cleveland."

Gabrielle put her hand on my shoulder. "Get it together. This visit is only a couple of days. You never need to see these people again. Screw them if they cannot accept who you are now. Be yourself, the beautiful young woman I adore. Everything will be fine."

"I am going to telephone Jack before we board the flight to Cleveland and let him know we'll be arriving at his house in a couple of hours, depending on traffic. We'll grab a taxi to his home. Okay?"

"Great idea, go for it." Gabrielle knew me and understood that I wanted to avoid a meeting at the airport for many reasons.

As soon as Jack answered the phone, I knew something was wrong. Jack was very subdued. "Marci, I am glad that you called. We've been at the Cleveland Clinic for the past three days. The house is a mess and we have not started preparing for Passover. For the last three weeks we have been traveling to various cities, meeting with doctors, taking tests at hospitals, in hopes of finding a cure. I will tell you their findings when I see you in person. Helen isn't doing well, and nothing has been started to observe the holiday."

I stuttered, "That's terrible. How can we help?"

He sighed. "Somehow, we will make things work. I am sorry. This may not be the Passover you expected. Anything you can do to get the house in order would be appreciated."

"Let me help you by preparing the Passover Seder meals," I said. "Remember, I have Gabrielle here to help me. While in Europe, I learned how to cook from a French chef. I have experience in the kitchen."

I could hear the relief in his voice when he answered. "If you could handle the Seder food preparations, that would be a godsend. But we have not yet purchased Passover food, cleaned the house or anything."

"We'll take care of it," I said. "How do I get into the house?"

"Go to the garage door. On the side of the garage there is a numbered keypad. Type in the security code, zero, zero, seven, and the garage door will open. The door leading into the house is unlocked. There are keys for the house and car hanging on the side of the refrigerator. Make yourselves at home. We have prepared a bedroom for you two in the basement. There is a private shower downstairs and towels in the basement closet next to the bathroom."

I ended the call, looked at Gabrielle, and burst into tears. Gabrielle tried to comfort me, but I just shook my head.

"It's not just Helen," I said. "I am crying because I do not know what it means to prepare a house for Passover or to prepare a Passover Seder. My parents were very lax when it came to Jewish observances. How can I prepare food for the Seder when I know Jack and his family keep kosher and I do not know or have a clue what is or isn't kosher?"

"I will help you," Gabrielle said. "The first thing we'll do before we board the airplane is to call the local Chabad. I assume they have a facility we can access. Ask for the rabbi and hand me the telephone."

I wondered how she knew about Chabad. I didn't even know what Chabad was. What could Chabad do for us? I was stunned. She seemed so confident, as if she

162

had previously prepared a Passover Seder. But how and where?

I followed her directions, dialed Chabad, and asked for the rabbi. I handed the phone to Gabrielle. She talked to the rabbi and explained the situation: we were out-of-town guests assisting a Jewish family in need by preparing a kosher home for Passover, but we were clueless where to start and unfamiliar with local shops.

She gave Jack's address to the rabbi as we boarded the airplane and our arrival schedule. As she fastened her seatbelt, Gabrielle explained. "Chabad is an organization whose sole purpose is to bring Jews back to observe God's laws. So, if you want to keep kosher, Chabad will help you with the process. They will help us make Jack's kitchen kosher for Passover."

I was incredulous and stared at her. "How do you know about them? What else do they do?"

"That's a long story for another day and another time." An exhausted Gabrielle laid her head on the headrest and closed her eyes. I tried to remember what I could about Passover traditions, but soon, I too, fell asleep.

Chapter 22

We took a taxi to Jack's house and found an older model, blue and white van waiting for us in the driveway. Two rusted out mega-speakers were mounted on its roof. Painted on the side panels of the van were the words, Mitzvah Mobile.

As we exited the taxi and lugged our bags toward the house, an energetic figure opened the van door. I had never seen anyone like him before. I wondered how this scruffy, old, gray-haired man was going to help us.

His beard was long and desperately needed a trim. He wore thick glasses. He practically jumped up and down with excitement. His black coat opened wide as words of welcome poured from his mouth.

He yelled, "Shalom," with a wide grin and open arms. "Thank God, your travels have been safe. We have lots of work and very little time. My name is Rav Shalom ben Hashem."

"I am Marci, and this is my friend, Gabrielle."

In a loud, blusterous voice, "It is wonderful to meet both of you. Thank you for allowing me to share in your mitzvah."

I asked and he explained. "A mitzvah is a commandment from God to perform good deeds." With that, he raised his hands like Moses in the movie *The Ten Commandments*. Ten young men emerged from inside the van. The oldest was, maybe, seventeen. They wore black shiny dress shoes, neatly pressed black pants, and clean white shirts. Each of them sported a black fedora. Their tender white faces were sprinkled with peach fuzz, as they were obviously trying to grow beards.

I walked to the side of the garage door and entered the security code. The garage door lifted, as Jack said it would. Once inside the house, I turned on the lights. Rav and his crew were right behind me. Gabrielle and I carried our luggage into the basement.

The visitors neatly removed their hats and placed them one on top of the other on the living room couch. They carefully took off their suit jackets and hung them in the guest closet. Then, each of them reached into their bags to retrieve large aprons that they then wore.

Instinctively, without a word being spoken, each knew their task. One started clearing out the food from the shelves, one cleaned out the food from the refrigerator, one prepared a solution of soapy hot water to scour the refrigerator, and one started the oven's self-cleaning program. It was like watching a Dr Seuss book come to life.

The Rav's helpers worked like bees in a beehive. Without a word, the Rav beckoned us over. Cautiously, Gabrielle and I approached him.

He looked at us with his glasses perched halfway down his nose and asked, "Do you need kosher Passover food?"

My eyes popped open. "Yes, but I do not know what foods to buy and have no idea what dishes I should use for the Seders and the rest of the week. Where do I purchase kosher foods?"

His hand moved sideways in the air. He said, "I have prepared a list of the things you will need for the Seder. Here are sample recipes that my wife composed for you. You are free to call her with any questions. Here is her phone number. My driver in the van will take you to the kosher meat store and the kosher grocery store. It may be easier to shop there. However, I am not sure what foods are still left on the shelves, since Passover is only two days away."

Like mice, we scurried into the van and drove off to the stores. Gabrielle explained that the house had to be cleaned of food particles before we could cook the Passover meal. Together, we found the name of a bonded maid service. We called them from the van and ordered a complete house cleaning starting at ten a.m. the next morning.

The first stop was Tibor's Kosher Meats. We purchased two briskets, ten pounds of skinless chicken breasts, two capons, a shank bone and ground beef.

The next stop was Unger's Kosher Food and Bakery. We cleared the shelves of the remaining food items. We bought pre-made pie crusts, frozen apple kugels, spices, cereals, bakery goods, yogurts, plenty of eggs, and tons of other items. By the time our purchases were rung up, we had enough food for ten people for two Seders, and a week's worth of meals.

While we were gone, the rabbi and his team of students had cleaned the entire kitchen. Everything sparkled. Appliances looked brand new. The shelves and the refrigerator were free of every trace of food and dirt. Immediately, we started to organize our purchases into the empty cabinets and refrigerator. The rabbi and his exhausted crew left. We offered to give them money which they would not accept.

The rabbi said, "It was our pleasure."

Just as I thought we were done buying things, Gabrielle enlightened me. She said, "A kosher Passover home requires pots, pans, plates and silverware which are used only during this holiday."

We had no idea where Helen stored her Passover cookware and I was not going to bother her on the phone, with everything she was going through. I figured it would be easier on everyone to just spend the money. I took the car in Jack's garage and drove to the local Costco.

Last on the list was wine, the most important part of the Seder. We asked the liquor clerk to assist us in the selection of a quality, high-end kosher wine. I remembered sipping cheap concord kosher wines when I was a child. It was nasty. We selected a case of Israeli wine called Mount Tabor, which had won numerous wine-tasting awards.

At the register, Gabrielle joked, "Every religion should have a holiday that requires drinking four glasses of wine. The world would be a much happier place."

All I could say was, *Amen*.

We returned to Jack's and I went online and donated to Chabad. The rabbi's generosity had inspired me, and I promised myself going forward that I would try to perform acts of kindness to benefit others.

Once we were alone, Gabrielle and I sat in the living room, opened the first bottle of wine, and relaxed. "Now the hard work begins in earnest. We'll be busy from tonight until the Seders are over."

"Thank you for being here with me. You are truly a lifesaver."

The sun set and rose in Cleveland. Jack called to tell me that they were spending the night at Helen's side at the hospital. Gabrielle started the chicken soup. She knew exactly what to do without looking at the recipe. She placed the capon in a large pot with cut up onions, carrots, potatoes, olive oil and various spices. She simmered the soup at a low temperature, as she made the matzo balls. No chicken soup is complete without those round tender matzo balls, Gabrielle explained.

I began cooking the brisket. I learned at the Compound that if you cook a brisket three-quarters of the way through and then cool it in the refrigerator, adding brisket sauce, for twenty-four hours, it will be juicier and more tender when it's reheated on the day the meal is served. Sweat dripped from our foreheads as we worked at a feverish pace. We had to finish all the preparations before the family arrived home tomorrow.

We located tablecloths, napkins and a table leaf in the upstairs linen closet. The table opened in the middle. We inserted a wooden leaf to expand the four-seat table so eight people could be seated.

By three p.m., we were ready for tomorrow; the first night of the Seder. We showered and went out for an early dinner and a couple of drinks.

Chapter 23

Two hours before the first Passover Seder was set to begin, Jack and his family arrived at their home. Helen was noticeably weak and a bit jaundiced. Jack and the boys looked worn out. The cancer had eaten away at least fifty pounds of Helen's body's weight. Jack pushed her wheelchair into the house.

She looked at me and paused before recognition dawned on her face. Helen smiled and asked Gabrielle and me, "What can I do to help? I am so sorry you two had to go to all this trouble and work on my account."

We wheeled her into her kitchen, so she could see the status of our preparations. "Oh, my goodness, I cannot believe all the hard work you two girls accomplished!"

Her tears of gratitude flowed. That was all the thanks we could have hoped for. We told her about the rabbi's visit and explained about the food preparation we'd done for Passover.

Helen rolled her wheelchair into the dining room. Her eyes widened and sparkled. "What a beautiful table you have prepared."

Jack came over and gave me a big hug. Then he went to Gabrielle. No introduction was needed. He hugged her, too. Helen was not the only one in tears. I cried, as well.

Jack looked into Gabrielle's brown eyes and said, "It is a pleasure to finally meet you face-to-face. I cannot adequately express the gratitude that my family owes the two of you."

Jack's sons respectfully greeted us and went upstairs to their rooms. I sensed they weren't sure how to interact with their old friend Marc, since I now had breasts and was wearing a dress. I smiled and kept a stiff upper lip. But it was hard.

Jack grabbed my arm and walked me to the backyard. "Marci, you are a beautiful young lady and I support whatever decisions in life you will make. I cannot imagine what you have gone through. This year you have conquered many obstacles and proved yourself a strong woman." I thanked him.

Jack continued, "This morning, Helen woke up with more energy than she has had in months. The first thing out of her mouth was that she wanted to go home and celebrate Passover with her family. Without you and Gabrielle, her wish could not have been fulfilled. I will always be in your debt."

I saw Gabrielle through the kitchen bay window and motioned her to come outside and join us. We sat down enjoying the spring weather and talked for ten minutes or so.

I explained to Jack, "Gabrielle is the brains of this outfit. She deserves most of the credit. Gabrielle knew

171

what to do and I followed her directions. I would have accomplished nothing, if not for her. She knew to call Chabad. It was her idea to bring in the maid service."

"I hope you know how appreciative we are," Jack said. "And I plan to reimburse you for these costs." Gabrielle looked down to the ground and smiled modestly.

"Jack, if your firm's tickets are available, I was hoping the three of us could catch a ball game while we are still here. The Indians are playing the Yankees. Gabrielle has never attended a baseball game and I promised that I would take her to one."

"Sure, I will get you the tickets, but my availability depends on Helen and her health. If Helen is stable, I would love to spend an afternoon with the two of you. I haven't been to a game yet this season."

"We'd better get inside. I see Helen is getting ready to light candles."

Helen called Gabrielle and me over to the table where she had set up her holiday candlesticks. She held the unlit match in her hand and said, "It's a woman's responsibility to light the candles to welcome in the Jewish Sabbath and holidays. Please stand with me and repeat the blessings along with me."

We stood beside her.

She said, "Close your eyes and think of your loved ones as we say the words." She lit two candles and together we said the ancient prayer that women have said for thousands of years. Afterwards, everyone kissed and wished each other a good, sweet holiday.

The Seder started. Jack proceeded to share his insights into the meaning of the Seder and, with that, each of us read a single page from the Haggadah. Helen read the first page. Everyone had a turn. There were no young children at the table, so everyone joined in unison and sang the Four Questions together in Hebrew. I was surprised to see Gabrielle knew the rituals and sang along with us in Hebrew.

Halfway through the Seder we stopped the service to enjoy dinner. Jack's two sons, Brian and Brett, served the hard-boiled eggs and fish appetizers, followed by chicken matzo ball soup and the main course. Lively conversations ignited the atmosphere, and we sat for hours getting caught up and sharing stories.

Initially, Brian and Brett were quiet but cordial to me. I knew it would take time and hoped they would one day feel comfortable around me. By the end of the evening, they made me feel like their welcomed, adopted sister.

It was a wonderful first night of Passover. The rabbi was correct when he said, 'everyone is in good spirits after four cups of wine.' The meal Gabrielle and I cooked was a hit. We were exhausted! The boys offered to clean the kitchen.

The second Seder began with the warm spirits of the first evening. Everything was running smoothly, until the middle of the readings, when Helen stopped and looked at her two sons.

"Brian and Brett, no mother has ever been prouder of her sons than I have been of you. Each of you has special and unique talents. I know that each of you will succeed in life. I love you for being there with me these past two months. If anything should happen…"

"Mom, nothing is going to happen," the boys tearfully interrupted her in unison.

"Just in case, I need you two to watch over your father. Look at me, slobbering like an old woman. I can't believe I'm crying here at the Seder table."

Helen did not wake up the next morning. She died on her own terms, quietly, at home, with her family and after the last Seder. She had lived a short life; a mere forty-four years. Her death was only a month before her twentieth wedding anniversary.

In Jewish tradition, Helen was buried in a plain wooden casket that did not contain any metal. The ceremony took place the following day. Approximately fifty friends and family attended the burial. Unfortunately, many were out of town, since Passover coincided with spring break. The family had to wait until the holiday was over before they could sit Shiva, observing the seven days of Jewish mourning of a family member.

Jack had known Helen's days were numbered, yet he was clearly shaken. After Helen's funeral, he asked

Gabrielle to join him in the library. The two of them sat and talked for hours.

The Shiva arrangements took time to plan. Gabrielle and I prepared meals for Jack and the boys and helped coordinate with Helen's friends. The boys came into the kitchen while we prepared food.

Brian said, "We would like to thank you both for everything you have done for our family. You've been here almost every day and night working. My brother and I will take over today, why don't you two get out, go to town and enjoy yourselves. This is no way to spend your vacation."

I said, "That's a great idea. I want to go downtown and work out on the lakefront tomorrow. I was hoping to make a day of it and check out the Rock and Roll Museum in the evening. Is it okay if we take the night off too? I will have dinner prepared for the three of you. You'll just need to heat it and clean up afterwards. What do you think?"

"That sounds great. We could all use a break."

On Friday morning, Gabrielle and I dressed for a run along the lake. We jumped in the car. The first stop we made was to thank the rabbi again.

Once parked outside Chabad Synagogue, we donned modest wrap-around skirts and blouses over our running attire. We walked into the building and asked for the rabbi. He came out of a classroom and, upon seeing us, greeted us with an inviting smile.

I returned his greeting. "Rav, thank you for seeing us. I wanted to tell you that Helen, Jack's wife, came home from the hospital to spend her last days celebrating Passover with us. She passed away after the second Seder. If not for you and your students… well, you know what I am trying to say." My voice cracked with emotion.

Gabrielle chimed in. "May God bless you and your students."

The Rav replied, "May her memory be for a blessing." He looked at Gabrielle and lifted his wire-rimmed glasses off his nose. "Do I know you from somewhere?"

She shook her head. "I don't think so."

The rabbi responded. "I think, in time, we will be friends."

The next stop was to apply for a new driver's license at the Department of Motor Vehicles. I wanted my driver's license to match my new name and gender. I used Jack's home address as my current residence. I stood in front of a solid blue curtain to have my unflattering ID photo taken. After I was issued my new card, Gabrielle and I stopped at Bloomingdales, where we picked up clothes appropriate for the Shiva. Two dressy black skirts, one with pleats and one with a slight slit in the front and matching jackets with three-quarter length cuffed sleeves to complete the look. I added two button-down silk long sleeved shirts. I found the most gorgeous pair of three-inch high heels and a black fedora hat. No one who knew me as Marc would recognize me in these outfits.

With our purchases safely stored in the car's trunk, we took a three-mile run and then joined a yoga class at a studio downtown. We showered at the studio facility and drove to the Rock and Roll Museum. There were floors of exhibits highlighting different genres of music and memorabilia. We spent hours there. Afterwards, we walked back toward the lake to Nuevo, a modern Mexican restaurant. There, we ate an amazing meal, filled with fusions of fruits combined with Mexican and Latin flavors.

In the car ride back to Jack's I asked, "Gabrielle, I noticed you and Jack talking in the library yesterday for some time. I'm curious, how is he doing?"

"He is a troubled soul. He knew Helen was dying, but he hoped it wouldn't happen. He loved her so much that he prayed for a miracle. Yesterday, he needed someone close to his age to talk with and to bare his soul to. So, I listened. He shared how he and Helen met and the early years of their marriage. He also knows what I went through, suffering the loss of someone I loved, so we discussed how I coped with Cristina's death. I told him that I still miss her."

We arrived back home hours before sundown. We started dinner and, at sundown, I said, "Do you think it's about time to light the Sabbath candles?"

I called the boys and Jack to come downstairs. Gabrielle joined me in lighting the candles and saying the blessings. As the women of the house, it was now our task. We sat down and enjoyed a traditional family Friday night dinner. A place was set for Helen. She was in our prayers and in our hearts.

Chapter 24

Hundreds of people came to pay their respects during the Shiva week. Outwardly, Jack and the boys appeared to be handling Helen's death reasonably well, but we knew the truth; they were hurting. This was the first time Jack was compelled to sit and talk with his friends and strangers about Helen's life. He struggled. He would have preferred being left alone with just his family around him.

Nobody recognized me, but I did get some flattering stares. I introduced myself to people as 'a family friend who flew into town'. I even had conversations with people I had previously known and was surprised when they did not recognize me.

Three days later, but before the crowds of people arrived, Jack was sitting in the family room on the brown leather couch. Gabrielle and I were in the same room performing yoga exercises.

Jack called out, "Marci, may I show you something?"

Gabrielle and I walked over and sat down next to him. Jack had a bag and a box in his hands.

"What's this?" I asked.

"I did not sell everything as you instructed me to do. I was planning to give these to you on your wedding day. I decided to hold on to your mother's jewelry box. I believe your mother would have wanted you to have it. I am hoping there may be something in there with some sentimental value. Here are your mother's Shabbos candlestick holders. Maybe you and Gabrielle will use them in your home together."

I got the impression from Jack's tone that he assumed that Gabrielle and I were lovers. I chose to ignore the inference. Now was not the time to correct him. Instead, I reached over to Jack and gave him a hug. I said, "I can't believe how thoughtful you are. My mother would have loved to see me wearing her jewelry."

The tears in my eyes made the diamonds in the box sparkle. I took out my mother's pendant necklace and asked Jack if he would mind securing the clasp for me. I told him, "My mother wore this pendant every day of her life. It was a special gift from my dad to her. Feeling it around my neck makes me feel close to her again."

Shaking off these precious moments I said, "We are returning to London in a couple of days. Join us at tomorrow's baseball game. Please, no excuses. You need to breathe some fresh air. We'll be back at least an hour before any of the Shiva guests arrive." He smiled and nodded his head.

The next morning, the three of us climbed into the car, ready to drive to Progressive Field to watch the

Indians play. I suggested to Gabrielle that it might be chilly at the park and maybe she should bring a light jacket.

She ran back into the house. I leaned over to Jack. "I thought you should know that Gabrielle and I are not romantically involved." I paused as I got a little emotional. "She is my best friend and has been like a mother to me since... She was once engaged to a male doctor who left her at the altar, before she met Cristina."

I could tell he felt awkward and wanted to change the subject. He cleared his throat and said, "Your mother's diamond pendant looks pretty on you."

"She truly loved it. It was her engagement present, a simple single diamond, on a silver chain. It will forever be special to me, knowing how Mom cherished it. It's a symbol of my parents' love for one another," I said.

Out of nowhere Jack asked, "Is Gabrielle Jewish? She has a kind heart and soul."

"I want to say no, but I have never asked her. She freaked me out when she read Hebrew at the Seder. She knows more about Jewish holidays and observances than I do. She told me to contact Chabad and the rabbi even thought he knew her."

"Her inner beauty transcends her physical attributes."

That afternoon, Jack sat and explained the game of baseball to Gabrielle. They drank some beers, laughed, and acted like lifelong friends. It was the best medicine for his broken heart. By the time we left the park, something told me that Jack would survive Helen's passing.

On the way to the airport, I reflected on the past few weeks in Cleveland. So much had happened. Jack and the boys loved me like a member of the family and regretted my leaving. We embraced at the airport. I was just two weeks away from my gender reassignment surgery. Jack said his goodbyes and promised to visit in four or five weeks to see how I was convalescing.

Chapter 25

By the time we got back to London, I had a renewed zest for life. The burden of uncertainty dissipated. Waiting for me were two pieces of mail: the acceptances from the University of Cambridge, and from Northwestern University McCormick School of Engineering. I had my choice and whatever path I took would change my life forever. I needed to discuss it with Jack and Gabrielle.

I continued to prepare for the surgery. I'd already had a laser treatment to deaden the hair follicles from the skin that would eventually be the lining of my vagina.

Gabrielle ruffled my hair as I scanned the acceptance letters over morning tea. "Morning, star shine. In two days, it will be the big day, surgery with Dr Mino on Monday morning. Put the toast down, you're on a strict fruit and veggie diet until you're recovered. Finish packing. We need to leave for the Compound in an hour."

Gabrielle reassured me while I finished breakfast, "Dr Mino has performed more than five hundred sexual reassignment surgeries. As we have previously discussed, he will use the penile inversion technique by inserting your penis into your body cavity. The nerves from your penis head will be placed in your new clitoris. The skin from your penis shaft and scrotum will be transformed into a vagina. Any questions? If no, get into the shower. If yes, you can save it for the doctor."

We left that afternoon and arrived at the hospital later that same day. I was shown to a pre-surgical room where I was asked to don a hospital gown while a nurse took my vitals. Gabrielle, the mother hen, nervously told me not to worry. She held my hand to provide me comfort. The next morning the anesthesiologist came into the room and administered something into my IV. I started to get woozy.

Gabrielle's voice followed me as I was wheeled down the corridor. She called out, "Sis, I will be waiting right here for you. See you after the surgery."

They rolled me down the clinic's sterile white halls. I could see the bright lights fading away. The anesthesia took effect, and the last thing I remembered were the doctors saying something to me.

I woke up after surgery and found Hilda and Gabrielle in my recovery room. My mind was unable to focus on anything. Everything was a blur. I was so cold, my entire body had goosebump shivers. Gabrielle saw my teeth chattering and covered me up with another heated blanket.

The doctor came into the post-op recovery room. His surgical mask was wrapped around his neck. He wore green scrubs and spoke in a heavy Belgian accent.

"The surgery went well. It lasted about three and a half hours. You must lie on your back for the next two days with your hips raised and legs apart to reduce the swelling. On the third day, you will be turned on your side. On the fourth day, we will remove the drainage tubes, packing and clean out the wound. If there are no complications, you may go home on the fifth day. Do you have any questions?"

I was still groggy, under the effects of the anesthesia and did not understand a word he said. I fell back asleep and dozed off for another two hours.

Eventually, I awoke. "Are you with us?" It was Gabrielle, whispering as her hand caressed my cheek.

I looked up at her and asked, "What are all these things tying me down?"

"You must stay in this position for the next two days to reduce swelling. The doctors placed drainage tubes inside of you to allow your body to drain the discharge from the operation. You have a Foley catheter to eliminate the urine and compression pads are pulsating around your lower legs. The comprehension pads prevent blood clots from forming. You have IVs providing your body with various medicines and needed liquids. Medical monitoring devices are attached to your finger and arm to monitor your vitals like blood pressure and heart rate. More importantly, how do you feel?"

"I guess I feel good," I mumbled.

Gabrielle laughed and said, "That's because of the drugs. You will feel differently when they wear off."

Packing maintained the shape of my vagina and kept it open after surgery. On the fourth day, the packing and the catheter were removed. The pain was acute, but I was able to tolerate it because of the drugs. Gabrielle told me that she would be quickly weaning me off the painkillers. She knew that they could be addictive over time, and she sought to protect me from forming an opioid dependency. Healing took a long time and the swelling persisted for months.

A week after my operation, we returned home for an extended recovery. The instructions dictated no exercising. I would be permitted to walk only when necessary for the first three weeks after surgery.

The operation knocked the shit out of me. I had no energy, and the dilation process, which started on the sixth day, was pure torture. I cannot describe the pain of inserting a foreign object into my newly created vagina. I dilated four times a day for the first eight weeks. I worked my way up from a one-inch diameter to a one-and-a-half-inch diameter dildo. The pain gave way to discomfort and, finally, became routine. Fluids continued to drain from my body during this first month. Without Gabrielle caring for me, I simply would not have been able to manage it. She showed me tricks that made the recovery and the dilation process easier.

Gabrielle reminded me of the need for the dilation. "The dilation process must be performed for the rest of your life. After six months, you will be required to dilate once a week. Intercourse can be a substitute for dilation."

Intercourse was the last thing on my mind. For the first three weeks I only had the energy to eat, dilate, clean myself and sleep. My body craved sleep, nature's way to recover from the surgery.

I was three weeks post-op and started performing tasks around the flat: cooking and light cleaning. I had a strict dilation time schedule and I still needed my naps to replenish the energy in my tired body. I had daily discharges, pain and depression. I was glad that I had had the surgery, even if the rehabilitation process was overwhelming.

Jack eventually arrived in London. He looked healthy and I appreciated him making the journey. I had hoped to have the strength to enjoy his visit by entertaining him at local restaurants and showing him the sights. Unfortunately, I was not up to it and Jack's schedule only permitted a week-long visit to London. I felt guilty about greeting him in my bathrobe and I wasn't wearing make-up. I looked terrible, but he understood.

We chatted for two hours, until my exhausted body gave out. I pleaded, "Do me a favor. Gabrielle has been locked up with me for days. Take her out for dinner, please. Gabrielle, get out of here, have a good time. Show Jack around town."

I shooed them out of the flat and lay down on the sofa. I was comfortable knowing the two of them would enjoy the evening together. I hoped Jack would learn to enjoy life again, especially after he'd put his life on hold for over a year as he cared for Helen.

For the next three nights the two of them went out after making me dinner. Gabrielle returned home that third night before midnight and promptly walked into my bedroom. I had been sleeping for hours.

She whispered, "Marci, are you awake?" I opened my eyes and tried to focus.

Seeing this, Gabrielle proclaimed, "I think Jack likes me. Wake up, so I can talk with my best friend."

I sat up, opened my eyes wide, and hugged Gabrielle. I encouraged her to tell me more. "So, do you like him? Are you attracted to him? Any apprehensions?"

She sighed and said, "He lives so far away."

I looked at her. "Duh."

She continued. "He is twelve years older than me."

I replied, "So what? You like older men."

Smiling, she confessed, "He *is* cute and doesn't want any more children."

"So, what's the problem? You are a perfect match for each other," I said. "Now, tell me every single thing that happened this evening. Start from the beginning! I want to hear every juicy detail."

Gabrielle giggled. She said, "You know I have been showing him the sights. We had some nice dinners and we even took in several theatrical performances. You know me. I avoided any questions he had about my

188

childhood. I did share that my father died when I was young, but that's all. I mentioned that I was a tomboy growing up."

"You are talking a mile a minute," I said with a tremendous smile on my face.

She was excited and chattered like a schoolgirl. "At dinner, he touched my hand. Afterwards, he reached for my hand while we were walking. I think he wanted to kiss me as I got out of the taxi."

"What did you do when he touched your hand?"

"I gave it to him."

"What did you do when he tried to kiss you?

"I gave him a hug instead."

I mulled this over. I said, "Gabrielle, do you like him?"

"He is a kind man. He could be a great friend and companion. This sounds stupid, given the limited time I have physically spent with him. Yet, sometimes you meet someone, and you have that feeling, like you could love that person forever. As I have gotten to know him, I believe that Jack is that person. Will you approve, if I get romantically involved with him?"

I grinned. "Go for it. It sounds like you have already fallen for him. The two of you need each other. If it works out, it would be great."

Gabrielle sighed happily. "I think I am going to kiss him tomorrow. Let's see what happens. I hate that he lives three thousand miles away, I wish distance wasn't an issue."

Over the coming weeks, and months, Jack and Gabrielle found that telephone calls were no replacement for the human touch. They were faced with a challenge. Would they let their relationship continue to grow or wither?

As Jack and Gabrielle got closer, I slowly continued my self-care. I received flowers from Fiora on my one-month post-surgery anniversary. She included a note which offered me words of encouragement.

On the eighth week after surgery, I elected to have an outpatient procedure known as a labiaplasty. This was an elective plastic surgical procedure to create a hood over my clitoris. Now, the appearance was complete. It looked like the real thing. After three months, I could resume riding my bicycle and swimming.

Chapter 26

I now had another decision to make. Which university should I attend? The time to send in my paperwork was due.

Gabrielle peered at me. She wanted the truth. "Marci, why do you wish to attend Cambridge when you could go to Northwestern? Didn't you tell me that Northwestern was your dream school?"

I was the baby bird, unwilling to leave the nest. I knew no one in Chicago, but that didn't scare me. I thought for a second. Then, I came clean. "The Northwestern program would be most challenging. It would provide me with the most career opportunities with top tech companies after graduation. That is not to say that I don't love you, but London is not Cleveland or Chicago. I'm here because I want to be with you. I want to live with you forever."

Gabrielle's voice softened. Sadly, she said, "You have no choice. I want you to accept Northwestern's invitation. It's best for you and your future. Down the road, maybe I will visit the States on a regular basis."

"What secret are you keeping from me, Gabrielle?"

She had that guilty smile of hers, as she spilled the beans. "You caught me. I forgot to mention that Jack and I plan to vacation in Florida over the holidays this December. If you are on winter break, consider joining us? His sons may be there too."

"What's up with the two of you? You never mentioned anything to me. Why the secrecy? Are things getting serious?"

She took a deep breath. "Well, you know we talk or email each other every day. That's no secret. This vacation is important because Jack wants to see how the boys react when they see the two of us spending time together, romantically. Until then, we are keeping our options open. I am scared and hopeful at the same time. I planned to tell you once you decided on your university. I didn't want to influence your decision."

I booked my flights after informing the admissions office at Northwestern that I would be there for the fall term. I completed and submitted all the necessary forms online and called Jack for the necessary funds.

I boarded at Heathrow and flew directly into Chicago's O'Hare International Airport. Compared to Heathrow, O'Hare was larger and busier. With my luggage in tow, I stepped toward the curb and hailed a taxi to drive me to Northwestern, located in the northern Chicago suburb of Evanston.

I arrived at the campus midday to witness the gleaming eastern shore of Lake Michigan. In the distance, waves crashed against the rocks and, closer in, there were sandy beaches. I imagined a quiet, warm day with time between classes, studying on its shores with a slight breeze blowing on my face. The water looked clear, a turquoise blue as I observed students participating in water and beach activities.

The school was twenty miles from Chicago's downtown bars, museums and nightlife, so I could go out and enjoy myself at any time. Yet, Evanston was a quiet town. It was far enough from the city's ruckus to provide a small-town atmosphere. The university was located steps from downtown Evanston, which comprised dozens of fine and trendy restaurants, bookstores and small shops.

I took the elevator to the third floor of my dorm building. My room was on the east side of the structure. I would share the suite with three other female students. The layout provided each student a small, furnished bedroom with a bed, dresser and desk. The bedrooms were connected by a common area, which was furnished with two couches, reading chairs and a flat screen television. There were two metal desks along the walls between bedrooms. We all shared a single bathroom with a shower.

I arrived eight days before the start of school, the very first day the school permitted dorm occupancy. I desired to get acclimated with the school and the city because it was so new. Being the first to arrive, I took the room facing the lake. I was excited by the prospect of watching the sunrise over the lake each and every morning. I was starting to unpack when I heard a noise from the common area.

I called out, "Is anybody there?"

I came out of my room and found one of my new roommates. With a welcoming smile I said, "Hi, I'm Marci. I am so glad someone else came here early."

"My name is Davi. I'm glad to meet you. Love your necklace!" Davi told me she was accepted to the McCormick School of Engineering. She was born and raised in the Chicago suburbs.

"The pendant was Mom's," I said. "I love your sandals. Where did you get them?"

Before Davi could answer, two other girls entered the suite. Each of them carried suitcases and were accompanied by their parents. We helped them unload their belongings from the family cars and then get settled after their relatives left. We agreed to reconvene in an hour to grab dinner together.

My other roommates were Ariel and Beth. Ariel was from a northern Chicago suburb called Highland Park. She dreamed of being a world-famous investigative journalist. In my first two minutes with her, I noticed she was smart and assertive. Beth was from Milwaukee, an education major. She was more reserved and less talkative.

I sat on my bed and reflected on my new suite mates. I was surprised by the similarity in their personalities and physical appearances. All three had shoulder length brown hair and slender but physically fit bodies. Unlike me, they had recently graduated from high school.

I was struck by the real-world differences we had. I'd lost my parents, traveled to Europe, survived a terrorist attack, come out as a woman, and undergone gender affirmation surgery. In comparison, my dorm mates were discussing their prom dresses and how this was the first time they were away from mommy and daddy.

I assumed each was awfully smart, otherwise they wouldn't be here. Fortunately, they appeared to be individuals whom I could develop friendships with.

After a while, I poked my head into their bedrooms to get to know each one better. I quickly noticed I was the only one who didn't have posters and pictures of loved ones displayed. I had no photos, not even of Gabrielle.

Beth asked, "Where should I go to purchase my course books? If you know."

I responded, "I wrote a search engine program to identify the best websites and stores for the books."

Overhearing me, Davi asked, "May I look at your program?"

"Sure. My laptop is in my room. Its already on. Let me know if you have any problems. I can correct them." With that, she broke into a wide grin and slipped into my room.

Ariel, Beth and I sat on the floor and chatted about our lives and family. We were talking when Davi returned and said, "You did a great job writing the program. I have added local bookstores into your search results. We can discuss it later. By the way, would you consider being in my study group? I have two other girls from high school who are also in our engineering program already in the group. You will love them. What do you say?"

"Awesome, yes. I would love to. Thanks."

Ariel said, "Guys, what do you think about going to Union Pizza for dinner? It's a gorgeous night. Let's walk and sit outside in the beer garden."

I looked at Ariel and said," I thought the drinking age in Illinois was twenty-one?"

"Where are you from, girl?" she joked. "You don't have a fake ID? You must be a real Miss Goody Two-Shoes. Tomorrow, we will take you for your new Illinois driver's license and you will be twenty-one."

I wasn't going to argue. I responded by saying, "Yeah, I guess I have lived a sheltered life. Let's go, I'm hungry."

The next morning, Ariel took me to a grocery store owned by two Jordanian brothers. For one hundred-and-fifty-dollars cash, one brother took my picture. He retreated into a back room. Fifteen minutes later, I obtained my new ID. It said I was a female from Evanston, Illinois, old enough to legally drink.

The beginning of the school year was only five days away, and things were hectic. It was a busy week. We successfully crashed several fraternity, beer parties. We got in by showing them our fake identifications. I located my classrooms and acquired all the necessary books and supplies. I went jogging with my dorm mates along the lakefront and signed up for yoga classes at the YMCA two mornings a week. Finally, I ordered online some framed posters of Switzerland and the white cliffs of Dover to hang in my room. I asked Gabrielle to send me pictures of the two of us.

As the days rolled by, my roommates and I got familiar with each other and settled into a routine. We hung out together most nights and worked out together during the day. We shared personal stories, prepared food and drinks, and set rules for the suite. I was very fortunate to have great roommates.

Ariel and Davi announced that they wanted to hit the bars that Friday evening before our first week of the semester. Without an explanation, Beth asked if she could meet up with us later that night. She seemed to be hiding something, so the other girls teased her, by suggesting she must have a secret boyfriend. She laughed it off and went back to her room.

I was concerned for Beth, so I knocked on her door. "Can we talk?"

She invited me to come in, so I sat on her bed. We chatted for a bit and then I asked, "Is there something wrong? Is there some reason that you don't want to go out with us?"

She laughed. "Not at all. I planned to go to Chabad for Shabbos dinner."

My hand instinctively covered my mouth as I digested what she just shared with me. I asked her, "Do you mind if I join you?"

I went back into the common area and told Davi and Ariel I was going to hang with Beth and promised to meet up with them later.

"Davi, if you go to a different place, text me and let us know where you are. We should be able to meet up with you no later than nine, maybe earlier."

I lit the Friday night Sabbath candles using Mom's candle holders which were displayed on the windowsill. I used shorter candles due to safety concerns. I didn't want to leave the room while the candles were still lit. Beth stuck her head into my room. I asked her, "Do you mind if we leave for Chabad in ten minutes, after my candles are out?" I had begun lighting them every Friday night after my visit to Cleveland.

Once the candles were extinguished, we walked to the Chabad house, which was located on Orrington Street. It looked like one of the fraternity houses. The rabbi greeted us like we were his long-lost cousins. He introduced himself as Rabbi David and told us that he was happy to see us. He asked for our names, majors and hometowns and offered to introduce us to hometown students. He seemed to know someone from every city. He made me feel comfortable and welcome.

We started to walk around the crowded house and introduced ourselves to other students, as the rabbi was in a mad dash to greet as many students as possible.

Beth and I were pushed into a crowded room and became separated. I instinctively walked into the kitchen. There stood a petite woman in a full-length dress and protective apron. I thought she might be wearing a wig.

With a smile, she said, "My name is Shoshana. I am the rabbi's wife. May I help you?"

I was excited to hear her accent and replied to her in French. She complimented me and said, "Were you born in France? If yes, where did you grow up? Did you attend the Jewish day school?"

I continued the conversation in French. "My name is Marci. No, I lived and worked in Europe last year. If you don't mind, I would appreciate having conversations with you in the future to keep my language skills fresh."

"I would enjoy that," she said.

I continued, "As for day school, I didn't have a great Jewish education growing up." I almost told her that my studies ended after my Bar Mitzvah. Then I offered, "May I help you in the kitchen?"

"I would appreciate your assistance, but we must work and talk at the same time." Shoshana leaned over and said, "There are many hungry students tonight. According to Jewish law, the food must be fully cooked by the time we light candles. The rabbi will then say the traditional blessings over the wine and bread. Afterward, we will serve appetizers and dinner."

Shoshana asked me to call her 'Shosh'. I agreed and asked if she would teach me more about the Jewish faith and Jewish observances. She was excited to help me discover my Jewish roots. I offered to come back every Friday afternoon after class to volunteer and assist her with the cooking. I told her I would make it work with my study schedule, since this was my first year.

Shoshana and the Chabad atmosphere made me feel comfortable. She allowed me to explore the path of my personal journey at my own pace. The Chabad house became an important place for me. Occasionally, I stopped there between classes to quietly study, rather than walking back to the dorm. I found cooking was a relaxing diversion from the school grind.

As time passed, Shosh and I became very close friends. I could always count on her when I had a problem. She would stop whatever she was doing and listen to my problems over a cup of coffee. She taught me Mediterranean cooking, Jewish traditions, and the significance of being Jewish. I hoped that Shosh would always be a part of my life.

Most Friday nights, Beth and I had Sabbath dinner and then joined our roommates for drinks and late-night fun. One night, the four of us were at the local bar, talking and drinking. A guy sporting a wide grin, came up to Ariel. She introduced him to the group. They chatted for a bit and tried to slip away, without a goodbye. Before she escaped, I stopped her by tugging on her arm.

Ariel shrugged me off. She told us she would meet us back in the room later or call so we wouldn't worry. We giggled as she disappeared with her crush.

That was the last time we saw her before the next morning. She thought she could sneak into her room before anyone noticed, but when she opened the door, we were already talking in the common area.

With raised shoulders and a sheepish smile, she said, "Oops, I guess I was a bad girl."

"Did you have a good time?" Davi asked.

Ariel confessed. "He was a guy from high school. We were friends and I always had a thing for him. He kind of knew, but nothing ever happened then."

"So, do you think there is a chance now?"

Ariel smirked mischievously. She said, "If you don't mind, I am going to my room so I can close my eyes for a few hours."

During our first year, I was the only one in my group who seemed to have no sex drive. I was also the only one who did not have a boyfriend at one time or another. I was so busy with school, Chabad, and my new friends that I didn't need a lover. Dating wasn't a priority. My life was very palatable and uncomplicated. I was becoming the person I always wanted to be.

The only person I missed was just an email away. Frequently, I shot off a message to Gabrielle and she kept me up to date with her life. Gabrielle was initially reluctant to tell me but after a little coaxing she told me that Jack and she were romantically inclined and pursuing a serious relationship.

Chapter 27

Classes at Northwestern were challenging from day one. Professors expected the students to have read and understood their initial reading assignments before the first day of class. Thankfully, Davi and her high school friends included me in their study group. The other two girls were Chinese, their names were Xuan and Su. They impressed me with their work ethic and knowledge. Together, we tackled every assignment the professor could throw at us. Our projects and hard work earned us the highest grades. We had stiff competition, but our study group was the best and others begged to join us. We told them no.

During the school week, the four of us worked on schoolwork but on the weekends, we often hung out together and got wild, but not drunk or crazy.

Ariel wanted to fix me up with someone. "There is a cute guy in one of the frat houses. He would like to ask you out. Are you interested? He is very good looking."

I didn't know if I was attracted to guys, but I did not want my roommate to know. I said, "I would love to go out with him but not this semester. My grades and career are more important right now. Maybe in spring."

Ariel rolled her eyes. "Come on," she said. "You can have both! Grades and a love life."

I shook my head. "Thanks for thinking of me, but I have to get through midterms." I knew Ariel was right. There was time for both.

Gabrielle and Jack took off and spent the winter vacation alone in Florida. I went to Mexico along with Brian and Brett. We had two rooms at an all-inclusive resort.

After a brief vacation I returned and slaved away until the next semester ended in June attentive to my studies. Given the choice, I remained on campus and enrolled in summer classes.

It was a Friday of my sophomore year and I was at Chabad talking and cooking for a crowd of fifty that night. It was late fall and the leaves had turned shades of burnt orange and yellow; my favorite season. Shosh and I were relaxed in the kitchen, conversing in French, thinking that everything was under control. The food was prepared and sitting in the ovens warming.

Shosh disclosed how her children coped with the fact they shared their parents with hundreds of students. In mid-discussion, a male student stepped into the kitchen. He stared at me, baffled to hear us conversing in a foreign language and said, "The rabbi wanted me to tell you the fifty men from the Sammy fraternity house are coming for dinner."

Shosh thanked the young man and shooed him out of the kitchen. We had less than one hour to cook the additional meals before candle lighting. Together, we worked as a team. We took chicken from the freezer, placed two pounds at a time in the microwave to defrost. As the microwave finished each batch, we took the meat and dunked the cut-up pieces in batter. We seasoned the poultry, threw it into the oven, and baked it. We made boxed mashed potatoes and reheated the soup, throwing in additional sliced potatoes, carrots, onions and water. We steamed the cold broccoli by placing it in strainers over the soup that was simmering on the stove.

When the rabbi announced it was candle lighting time, I wiped the sweat off my face and congratulated Shosh that we pulled off a miracle. Shosh and I laughed out of sheer relief.

That fall semester was a whirlwind. Thanksgiving arrived quickly, just when I needed a break. I had been devoted to my studies for three months and was looking forward to an extended weekend away from my books. Davi and Beth invited me to come home with them to celebrate the holiday, but I already had plans. I was looking forward to preparing Thanksgiving dinner for Jack and the boys. I was the lady of their house.

When I asked Ariel what she was doing over fall break, she was coy and evasive. I pressed her when we were alone. She said, "My parents are in California, I'm planning to stay in the dorm and grab something in town. No big deal. I prefer it that way."

"Like hell you do! You are coming with me to my uncle Jack's house in Cleveland. Nobody should be alone for Thanksgiving. If it's a question of money, I will pay for your flight. You will have a wonderful time."

"Are you serious?" she said. She gave me a shy smile. "You're the best."

While she packed her bag, I called Jack. "I hope you won't mind I invited a friend for Thanksgiving," I said. "She has no place to go."

"Great! Love to have her."

"Jack, I'm cooking dinner. I have composed a shopping list of food and spices I will need when I arrive to start preparations. Please don't argue with me. I'll email the items to buy as soon as I hang up."

"Are you sure, Marci? That's so much work," he said. "Of course, we appreciate eating home-cooked meals. Truthfully, I think the boys are getting tired of my cooking and take-out."

"I'm happy to do it," I said. "We are family. Hugs and kisses, see you soon."

Brian picked us up at the airport. He gave me a meaningful hug. He saw Ariel and broke into a covert smile. I thought he was going to stand there all day and stare at her before he got back into the car.

When we got to Jack's house, Brian ran upstairs. Two minutes later, he called down to me. "Marci, I need to show you something." I left Ariel who was talking to Jack and went to Brian's bedroom. I thought to myself that Brian was behaving oddly.

206

"Why all the cloak and dagger?" I asked as I stepped in his room.

Instead of answering me, he asked, "Is she dating anyone?"

I played stupid. "Who, me? I'm not dating anyone."

"No, is Ariel dating anyone?"

"She's not dating anyone now. Are you interested? She is very cute and awfully smart."

He smiled with delight at my answer. We went downstairs to join the others. Although he took part in our conversation, Brian's eyes were only on Ariel for the rest of the day.

As I prepared dinner, Ariel joined me in the kitchen. I had my hands in the bird when I noticed she was no longer in the kitchen. I peeked into the living room and saw her laughing and giggling on the couch with Brian.

Seeing me alone, Jack volunteered to help me with the food prep. It gave us an opportunity to talk and catch up.

I must admit, my turkey turned out perfectly. Cooking it upside down allowed the fatty juices of the bird to settle in the breast, making the white meat extra juicy. Yams and sweet potatoes melted in everyone's mouths. Everyone enjoyed and appreciated every morsel of food.

After dinner, Jack invited me into the family room. I sat in Helen's red leather reading chair as Jack stoked the wood in the fireplace. "Marci, it wasn't so long ago,

Helen cooked Thanksgiving dinner for a house full of friends and family. My parents, your parents, and Helen are no longer with us. They all died too young." He looked sad enough to cry.

I comforted him, saying, "You're not even forty-six yet. You're too young to be talking like an ancient soul. You have many good years to live. The boys will get married and have children that you'll want to spend time with."

"Of course, you know Gabrielle and I are becoming very good friends." I nodded my head and my eyes twinkled.

In the background, I heard laughter and water splashing as the boys rinsed the dishes before placing them in the dishwasher. Ariel cleared the table and then joined in on the fun in the kitchen.

After a wonderful, but too-short holiday, Brian drove us to the airport and pulled into the loading zone. Ariel got out of the car and she and Brian embraced with a kiss. As I stood on the curb, Brian handed me my bag and kissed my cheek. He drew me close and said, "Thank you for bringing Ariel and cooking a great dinner."

On the airplane, Ariel peppered me with questions. I answered the most important ones, assuring her that Brian was a good guy, someone she could trust.

Chapter 28

The coming week, the fierce winter started to raise its ugly head. I quickly learned why people call Chicago, the Windy City. It would have been more appropriately named 'The Cold, Wet, Icy, Snowy, Horribly Windy City'."

There were two more weeks of classes before exams and then winter break. I was an A-student and sought to reward myself in Florida's warm weather. I was planning to meet up with Jack and Gabrielle in Miami and then take a two-day excursion to Orlando. I wasn't sure if the boys were joining us.

All my dorm mates were headed to different destinations, or so I thought. While waiting for my flight, I noticed Ariel by my gate.

I called out to her, "Are you on my flight to Miami? Why didn't you tell me?"

She blushed and said, "Brian asked me to join you and the family, but he made me swear to keep it a secret. I felt bad not telling you, but he made me promise."

"Don't worry. It's wonderful you are joining us in Florida. We'll get to spend some time together. I love it that the two of you are enjoying each other's company."

Jack booked four rooms at the Betsy-South Beach Hotel on Ocean Drive in Miami. It was even nicer than the place I'd stayed in Switzerland. Brett and Brian shared one room, Ariel and I shared another, and Jack and Gabrielle each had their own rooms. Jack was still concerned that his sons wouldn't understand if he shared a room with Gabrielle, eighteen months after the passing of their mother.

December in Miami was warm. The sun was bright. My pale skin badly needed those hot, humid sunny days. I saw little of Gabrielle and Ariel except at dinner. The couples abandoned me, so Brett and I lounged on the beach or hung out poolside. For the first two nights we only saw the two couples at dinner. Afterward, they vanished again, so Brett and I hung out at the bars together.

On the third day, Ariel and Brian joined Brett and me all day. Together, the four of us went parasailing, rented water scooters, and sipped margaritas by the pool.

Jack and Gabrielle joined the rest of us for breakfast and dinner most evenings. They were inseparable. Sometimes, I would run into them strolling on the beach, holding hands. They were deeply engaged in one another. I am not sure if Gabrielle used her room for sleeping.

After breakfast, two days before leaving, Gabrielle apologized for not spending enough time with me. "Can you forgive me? Can we talk?"

"I understand. No worries. What's up?" I said.

She blurted, "I think I'm in love again. Jack is in love with me, too. He asked me to move to Cleveland. I am scared. Should I give up all that I have worked so hard for, including my position at the hospital, for a possible romance?"

"You deserve to be happy in a loving relationship. You have been alone for too long. This could be your one chance to be with your soulmate. We will see much more of each other if you lived in the States. The real question is, are you willing to start over and make new friends? Can you get a nursing position in the States? What about the flat?"

"I love my friends," Gabrielle admitted. "But I have no one in my life since Cristina. I would like to take the risk. However, Jack will only marry me in a Jewish ceremony, meaning I would have to convert."

"I thought you were Jewish!" I said. "You know so much."

"Harold was Jewish, so I took a year of conversion classes. For two years I kept a Jewish home when I lived with him."

Gabrielle asked me about my love life, I told her the truth. "I have no libido and feel no physical attraction to anyone. For now, I am perfectly satisfied being with my friends."

Gabrielle said, "You will find love in the proper time. It's more important to have good friends than bad lovers. Wait until you meet the right person. You will know that person the moment she or he comes into your life. I am certain my life and heart belong in Cleveland with Jack."

Chapter 29

The plane from Miami brought us back to Chicago's frigid weather. Ariel slept most of the flight. Before dozing off, she admitted, "I have a crush on Brian. He said he loves me."

I thought to myself, "*Why would anyone want to live in Chicago during this time of the year, when the city is covered with snow and ice?*"

We finished finals and started the spring semester as winter's cold grip slowly relented to warmer weather. As the snow melted, buds appeared on the trees and tulips began to blossom all over campus. The semester ended and all my close friends were in relationships.

Davi, Beth and Ariel took off for the summer. Before summer break, we tentatively agreed to sign an apartment lease in fall.

I stayed in Evanston in a sublet apartment and spent the summer riding, studying and reading for pleasure. I just wanted to chill out. Every other weekend I spent time with Jack and Gabrielle either here or in Cleveland.

During the summer, I received a text from Beth: 'In love, parents adore him. We might get a place together in fall. Sorry, will miss the gang.'

Davi was the first to respond to Beth: "So happy for you. I'm having a great time in California; want to live here. Partying nearly every night. See the rest of you in fall."

Ariel responded with a sad face: "It was a blast while it lasted. My boyfriend, Brian, will be transferring to Northwestern. We are getting an apartment together." Gabrielle had already told me but I had waited for Ariel's announcement.

Love was definitely in the air. Fiora was dating an Israeli soldier and they were going to move in together. Her cousin got married and moved out of the apartment. Fiora confided, "I think that this may be the real thing. I still miss you and love you. I think of you often."

I missed her too, but I knew we were each in the right place, living the lives we were meant to live. However, I was unable to attract or be attracted to a lover and I was starting to wonder if I was destined to be without one for life.

My third year at Northwestern started as fall returned to Evanston. I was blindsided by the professor on our first day of class. "I have been impressed by the group comprised of Su, Xuan, Davi and Marci. Therefore, I have decided to mix up last year's teams. I am assigning a male student to your group and I am reassigning Xuan and Su to other groups. I may assign a fourth person to Davi and Marci's group in time."

I raised my hand immediately. "Professor, that's not fair. First, a study group is like a marriage, it requires compatibility. My partners and I are a great team. Breaking us up compromises our grades. Second, women are so much smarter than men. Why are you taking away my female study partners and giving us a male student? Why should we be responsible for teaching a guy, when that's your job? Why should I double my workload just for a guy to take credit for my efforts?"

The girls in my class vocally endorsed my statements. Others laughed. In my final plea, I asked, "Please allow our group to remain intact."

The professor looked at me with amusement. He said, "I understand your frustration with us. My wife tells me the same thing every night." The class laughed.

He continued. "In the real world, teams are broken up and members reassigned regularly. You need to be able to work on the team to which you are assigned. Even if you wind up on an all-male team, you must accept the assignment and do your best. That's the last word on the subject. Now, Adam, you are going to work with Davi and Marci. Good luck. Please do not disappoint these women. Try to keep up with them."

The students in the class chuckled as they stared at Adam. He placed a book in front of his face, not knowing what to say. He looked like he wanted to jump out of the window.

After class, Adam, Davi and I sat down on one of the cement benches outside to talk. We compared schedules and set study times when the three of us could meet to work on projects together. I laughed and told Adam, "You do know that I was kidding about men, don't you?"

He said, "Whether you were or not, this situation puts a lot of pressure on me. I hope I won't be a hindrance. It's such a handicap being a guy. Hopefully, you will cut me some slack."

I wasn't sure if he was angry with me or not.

He changed the subject abruptly. "Do you remember meeting me before today?"

I stared at his face for a moment. "No, I don't recognize you. Should I?"

Adam smirked and shook his head as he replied, "Sitting in the same computer engineering classes going on three years, I guess I made a lasting impression. By the way, are you French or American?"

Not missing a beat, I answered him in French. I said, "Are you sure you were in my class all year? You must be one of those shy, silent types." Then I reverted to English. "Do I look French, or is that the line you use with every girl?"

He was speechless. I wasn't sure if he liked my attitude. At first, I didn't care one way or the other. But there was something that intrigued me about him. It didn't hurt that he was handsome, even if he wasn't very outgoing. He stood about six feet tall, clean cut and was dressed in a button-down shirt and jeans. I learned from Davi who knew him from high school that he enjoyed sports and was a dedicated student. She didn't share he had recently broken off a relationship with a blonde sorority girl.

Saturday night at the bar, Ariel announced that this was her last girls' night out for a while. She made a commitment to spend the weekends with Brian. She promised to join us for yoga class once a week. The only time we talked was when I caught up with her every couple of weeks at Nails and More. And then she told me that Brian and she were talking marriage after senior year.

I knew that Ariel would make a great wife for Brian and an awesome mother. Part of me felt her slipping away. Of my original roommates I was closest with Ariel. Because she was my best friend on campus, I grabbed Ariel's arm and said, "Remember your girlfriends. I am your friend for life."

"If not for you, I would never have met Brian. You are an awesome friend. I hope we can always remain close. When you are ready, I know a guy who is dying to go out with you."

Chapter 30

I was at the store buying a bottle of wine and one of Adam's underage frat brothers approached me to buy a case of beer. I told him, "It will cost you. On the QT, what can you tell me about Adam?"

Halfway through the first can, he told me everything he knew. Adam had several relationships at Northwestern, but none of them lasted more than three months. Most were sorority girls who left him intellectually unsatisfied. He said, "Adam was looking for a challenge."

He opened a second can and continued. "Adam is a great guy. He grew up in Highland Park, he was a star on his high school's basketball team and is the best athlete in the frat house."

From what I learned, I needed time to consider if I wanted him as a boyfriend. I never considered myself attracted to jocks and playboys. They were too unstable.

Two weeks later, I was at Chabad cooking, when the door to the kitchen burst open. A student rushed in. It was Adam. He stopped dead in his tracks and, although his eyes were fixed on me, he spoke to Shosh. "The rabbi wants me to inform you that thirty guys from my fraternity are coming for dinner in an hour."

I looked back at him with a straight face. "Yes, I remember you now. You're the student who waits until the last minute to create more work for me. I hope you are not going to do this with our study group, too. Now, scoot out of here so the women can get to work."

He left looking like a punished puppy. I guess no one ever sassed him before. In French, I told Shosh, "I think he's cute. But I want to house train him before I take him home."

We laughed as we worked in fire drill mode to prepare the food needed. Once again, we were able to pull off a minor miracle with very little time to spare.

After dinner, I left and headed for home. I was planning to spend the rest of the evening alone with my books and music. My roommate, Davi, was at the bar and probably not due home until morning.

Suddenly, as I was halfway down the street, someone pulled on my arm. I was frightened. I could not speak or call out for help. I whirled around. It was Adam. He had to run to catch up with me.

"Don't walk so fast," he said in an apologetic tone. "Have I done something to offend you? You always seem so angry with me."

"Shit, you scared me." I paused to catch my breath. "Never sneak up on me again!"

He apologized for startling me. While I composed myself, I said, "You seem like a good guy. I am sorry if I hurt your feelings. It wasn't my intention to hurt you."

He said, "You can apologize by joining me at the frat for some refreshments." It wasn't exactly my idea of a relaxing evening, but I agreed. We walked together to the frat house. The music and the partying were so loud that I could hear it a block away.

"Adam, would you mind going to a quiet restaurant on Chicago Avenue instead? We could sit, talk and order a drink. I would like to get to know you better and besides we won't be able to talk at the noisy frat."

Adam liked the idea that I wanted to get to know him better, but he had some misgivings. He said, "I can't order alcohol. I am six months shy of my birthday."

"Come on, I'll buy you a Coke," I said.

We had a great time together and it turned out to be a wonderful evening. I learned that he had a good heart and found we were both avid baseball fans. He was a die-hard Cubs fan. Adam shared his fascination for the Cubs and his favorite moments from the last season.

We connected right away. I didn't really have any expectations beyond being friends. Things started off slowly and I did not get the sense that we were starting a romantic relationship. We did not kiss or hold hands. After that night we hung out, studied together, and I got to know him as a person.

He asked lots of questions about my family and my life before college. It meant a lot to me that he cared to ask. I selectively told him about Jack, my best friend,

Gabrielle and a year working at a European spa. I didn't mention the Compound.

On the weekends we went on outings, but they were as friends. On one Indian summer day when the weather was gorgeous, Adam and I rode twenty-three miles to the Museum of Science and Industry. The four-lane lakefront bike path accommodated hordes of walkers, skateboarders and bikers. Pedaling south at a quick pace, I was taken by the lake's blue waves and multitude of beach goers. Just past Oak Street Beach, the waves came crashing into the barrier wall and splashed us with refreshing, cold spray on this steamy-hot day. My eyes caught the majestic water, mirrored by the sunny azure sky.

By the time we reached the museum, I had painful calf cramps. I got off the bike and laid on the grass, in agony. I called out, "Adam, my calf muscles are burning, I need to rest."

He quickly dismounted from his bike and ran over to me. He began straightening out my legs on the ground. "Adam what are you going to do? It isn't going to hurt?"

He said, "Trust me. I know how to handle leg cramps. I've had my share of them." He made me sit up, pulled my toes towards me and I felt my calf muscles stretching. Then he massaged one leg at a time, starting with my right calf. My weary legs were soon free of cramps and pain. I enjoyed his touch and wanted to be closer. Together, we stretched in preparation for the return trip home.

Adam and I rode over to a drink stand on the beach and bought two bottles of Gatorade. We sat for a few minutes, enjoying the refreshing drinks and the beautiful view of the lake. We locked up the bikes, took off our shoes and strolled into the lake, knee deep. To be cute, I dipped my hand in the water, splashed him, and then tried to run away with the water resisting my efforts. Adam chased me down. He grabbed me from behind and I feared him tossing my entire body into the water.

I pleaded with him. "Please don't throw me in. I will be so embarrassed riding home in a wet sports bra."

But you know how boys are. He threw me in Lake Michigan! The water felt good. I pretended to be angry for two seconds before I started to laugh and then we headed back.

After the ride, I desperately needed to wash my hair and shower. A bicycle helmet isn't friendly to a girl's hair. I went back to my apartment and he to his place. Again, he didn't attempt any physical gesture of affection.

In the evening, Adam texted me and we agreed to grab a pizza. During dinner, Adam opened up to me for the first time. "I never want to become my father. He loves me, don't get me wrong. He is a workaholic. His work always came first. Our family was his hobby. I can't remember a vacation when my dad was not on the phone conducting business. I want a different life. When I have a family, I want to spend quality time with my children. I want to take an active part in their lives."

I internally questioned why he was telling me this. Every girl loves to hear the guy she's dating prioritizes family values. But we weren't romantically involved, although my heart was connecting more with him every day. I feared telling him that I couldn't have children. I didn't want him to leave me.

In October, we attended our first Cubs game together. Cleveland was experiencing a warm bout of weather. We sat on the third base side in the third row, just feet from the Cubs' dugout. They were fantastic seats. The stadium was packed. I bought him a beer or two. The Cubs were fighting for home field advantage in the upcoming playoffs.

"Adam, did you have any favorite Cubs players growing up?"

"You bet. D Lee, Kerry Woods and Ernie Banks. When I was fifteen or sixteen, I bought a ticket for opening day. None of my friends were willing to ditch school. I took the train from the Linden Station to Addison Street, which let me off at the ballpark. The man sitting in front of me was Ernie Banks. I recognized him right away. The seat next to him was vacant, so he invited me to join him. For two and a half hours, I listened to Ernie's stories of baseball and its legends. That was my greatest thrill ever."

"You mean being with me isn't your greatest thrill?" I teased. "What an awesome experience. I have no stories to compare with that one."

Adam asked, "Did you attend baseball games in Cleveland?"

"Before my parents died, my dad and I saw about ten games a year at Jacob's Field, and maybe one or two in other parks. Once a summer we traveled to New York and Boston for games. I was an only child, so they let me do almost anything I wanted. I was a tomboy when it came to sports."

"What did you think of those parks?"

"I loved visiting the stadiums in New York and Boston. The Green Monster in left field and the history in New York made me feel like I was standing on hallowed ground. My father loved baseball. We bonded over the game."

Adam said, "My dad promised to take me to a game, but he was always too busy."

That day, we ate and drank plenty and yelled and slapped high-fives every time the Cubs scored a run. During the seventh inning stretch, we stood and sang, 'Take Me Out to the Ballgame' with his arm around my shoulder as we swayed in unison.

I felt he shared his personal self because he trusted me. I was enjoying our time together but questioned how long could it last? At the end of the game, he took my hand and led me out of the park.

On the way back to campus Adam asked, "Can I see you tomorrow?"

I was surprised that he wanted to spend time with me so soon, but I tried to play it cool. "Sure, stop by. What do you want to do?"

"Can I surprise you?" When I nodded yes, he added, "I'll see you in the morning."

Sure enough, the next day, I awoke to a knock on the door.

I heard a voice in the hallway say, "Marci, are you up?"

I went to the door in my robe. My eyes were still partially closed, and I wasn't wearing any make-up. "Shh! Shh! What are you doing here? It's so early."

Adam was at my door. He said, "I thought I would surprise you. Join me for a bagel and coffee. I'm going to take you sailing on Lake Michigan. We'll be gone for a couple of hours."

Before I could wipe the sleep from my eyes, he handed me some gear. "Here is a wetsuit. Try it on. I hope it fits. I rented a sailboat. You said last night that I could surprise you, remember?"

"Give me fifteen minutes to clean up and change. I must really like you to trade sleep for cold lake water." I smiled and shook my head in disbelief.

Adam had rented an eighteen-foot sailboat. We went out on Lake Michigan. The lake was calm and the waves were not too choppy. The breeze caught the sails and it felt like we were gliding on clear ice. The spray splashed and made my hair frizzy, but it was totally worth it. I enjoyed everything about the sun, the wind, and my time with Adam. The day ended much too soon.

When we'd tied up at the dock, I hugged Adam and told him, "These last two days have been incredible. I can't believe you introduced me to my first Cubs game and a sailboat for the first time. I will always remember these wonderful experiences you have shared with me. Thank you again." On the way back I asked, "Would you mind dropping me off at the apartment, so I can shower and take a nap?"

He said, "No problem. I have not studied all weekend. After you shower and nap, can we go for a quick bite and study? I have a ton of school work."

"Yes, but only if we go to the library," I said. "I can't think straight. I am wiped out. The sun drained all my energy and I do need to nap."

Adam did not try to kiss me after any of our adventures which I found frustrating. Maybe he just saw me as his new buddy and harbored no romantic interest. I had no reason to assume we were more than friends. During my nap, I dreamt he held me and passionately kissed me, like those hot scenes in the movies. I enjoyed every minute of it. When I awoke, I realized he had become more than just a friend to me.

Winter break approached. Ariel was heading back to Florida. Davi and Beth were with their boyfriends, traveling to Mexico.

Adam came to my room on a Saturday morning. I expected him to pick me up later and didn't have my make-up on. When I opened the door, he handed me a package.

"I have a present for you. Call it a Hanukkah gift."

"Adam, I feel badly. I didn't buy you anything."

"Don't feel bad. I didn't buy you a gift looking for a gift in return," he said.

We sat on my bed and he handed me a box. I quickly opened it with anticipation. I pulled out the shirt, shook it out, and held it up. It was my own Cubs jersey.

I laughed and said, "Now, we can go to the games as a pair. Thank you so much!"

He grinned at me. I gave him a sincere hug and a kiss. It was our first kiss and, for the next five minutes, we were making out. I sensed when he patted my behind, he wanted more, but he seemed too shy and made no advances.

"Wait!" I said. "Only my first name is embroidered on the back of the jersey. I thought the last name was supposed to be on the back?"

"Girls tend to change their last names when they marry, so that's why I had your first name embroidered on it," he said.

I wrapped my arms around his back, closed my eyes and initiated another passionate kiss. This time shivers ran down my back and my legs. I had to catch my breath. We were definitely more than just friends, yet he didn't try to take me to bed.

In our last week of classes before winter break, my software engineering professor challenged the class to undertake an extra credit project. The assignment had to be successfully completed and submitted before the end of winter break to qualify for the credit. Then he said, "I don't think any of you have the skill or ability to solve this problem, but here it is. For the person or team who solves the problem they will receive my recommendation and a possible job placement opportunity with a Fortune 100 company."

Briefly reviewing the problem, it appeared beyond anything we learned in the classroom. With that said, I was determined to find the solution. I knew that I would need the assistance of another student or two. Finding someone who wanted to stay and work on it was a struggle. Most of my classmates had already decided to pass on the assignment for warmer climates. I didn't need the extra credit, but the recommendation and a job placement were inviting. I had to decide if I wanted to leave for winter break or slave away working on an impossible project.

I asked Davi and Adam if they would change their winter break plans to support my efforts. Davi expressed her regrets. "If I wasn't going to Mexico, I would stay and work on the project with you."

I hugged her and wished her safe travels. To my surprise, Adam volunteered to stay with me and work on the project. He cancelled his plans for warmer surroundings to stay in brutally cold Chicago to help me. Part of me feared our efforts could easily be a total waste of time.

After finals, Adam moved into my apartment with me. I demanded we get down to business and take the project seriously. At night we shared a bed. I wore shorts and a T-shirt, and he slept in his gym shorts. I admired his beautiful physique. He held me in his arms until he fell asleep, briefly touching my breasts. I assumed that he wanted to make love, but his hands went no farther than my breasts. I started to question whether he just didn't find me sexy enough for sex.

During the day, I ignored my feelings for him and concentrated on the assignment. I wanted him to feel it was our joint project, so I tried to take an equitable approach. I wasn't going to let him think that he was the brains of the outfit; instead, we'd work as a team. Guys like to think they are in charge, but I wasn't going to manage his ego on top of my other work. It was easier to just be partners.

"Adam, how do you think we should approach the problem?"

Adam thought for a minute and responded, "This is both a physics and software engineering problem. I suggest that we flowchart the various components of the issue. Then, we should discuss which components should be addressed and in which order of priority. We can create a flowchart matrix of the possible solutions to the various problems we detect and their possible solutions. Next, we will test the viability of each proposed solution. Once we have determined which theory appears to offer the optimum results, we can begin to write the program and test the solution with the computer."

I was impressed. Adam had developed a good method to solve the challenge. I asked, "What are the components of the problem, the variables that we need to identify in our solution? How do they relate to the problem as posed?"

Our methodology began to sync up. We were both getting excited, and it seemed like we had a chance to solve the challenge.

Adam said, "It's a usage of fuel, with multiple aircraft over a certain period of time."

"I agree." We were both strong in physics and addressed the variables of consumption, time and space.

"I like how you stated that. Let's focus on one variable at a time. Which one should we tackle first?"

I found we worked well together, neither of us had an ego. We defined the problem in the simplest of terms, used the flowchart to develop an action plan, and applied our theories to the computer to test them out. Together, we challenged one another, using critical thinking to find answers.

Each day, we spent six to eight hours collaborating. By the time we wrapped up each session, we were mentally exhausted, unable to think clearly. We took a break for dinner and, if we had the energy, we put in an extra hour or two afterwards or spent the night watching movies. Each of us wrote pieces of the program and worked on all aspects of the project. It was my responsibility to write the more difficult and technical portions. Adam would then review my work and test it for flaws. We made a terrific team. At night, I was hoping he would desire my body.

The next night, we walked to the closest restaurant. Adam reached for my hand and we held hands until we sat down. During our meal, he offered to share his fries. His right hand reached across the table to touch mine.

As our hands touched, he joked, "Wouldn't it be great to work on projects together after we graduate? We'd make great roommates, huh?"

I wanted a real relationship with this man and was hoping my kisses alerted him to that fact. I looked him dead in the eye and said, "I want to be more than just a schoolmate or roommate with you. I'm hoping for more."

His eyes widened and a grin appeared. Yet, he said nothing.

When he didn't respond, I asked, "Do you see me only as a roommate?"

I felt some apprehension asking the question. Had I misread the situation? He did not answer me immediately, which confused me even more. He avoided my question, so I let it drop. We returned home to catch a movie.

That evening, as we sat on the couch together, he put his arm around me. We selected a romantic comedy to watch. From the time we left the restaurant until the start of the movie, my mind was consumed with jumbled thoughts. I'd shown my cards. Now, I needed to know what kind of relationship *he* wanted with *me*. I had never been so frustrated in my life.

In the middle of the movie, I wiggled onto his lap, straddling him. My lips were six inches away from his. I knew I had his undivided attention. I opened my mouth to talk but, instead of giving him my well-reasoned explanation for why we should get involved, all I could do was kiss him.

Our passions were ignited into an uncontrollable force. He was eager and fully engaged. Finally, Adam was releasing his emotions with no reservations. At this point, everything happened much too quickly. I don't remember how my shirt and bra found their way onto the floor. My breathing was out of control and my heart was pounding. His hands and mouth were all over my breasts. I didn't want him to stop. I enjoyed the sensations that I was experiencing and was compelled to touch and explore his body.

His hands opened my pants. I felt his fingers and I was losing my grip on myself. The libido that I thought was non-existent was alive and well. My excitement had taken over my brain; I had no self-control.

I looked down at Adam's face, which was flushed with excitement. I wanted him, yet fear pierced me like an arrow. *Could I have sex? How painful would it be? I knew I was fully healed, but could he damage me if he was too large? My mind yelled to my body, 'Stop everything! We're going too fast'.*

Without a word I used my hands to push him away. I got off the couch with my pants near my ankles, even though both of us craved more intimacy. Stunned he went to the bathroom and ran the water in the shower. I dropped my pants and panties on the floor.

I wanted him and was afraid he'd perceive my retreat as a rejection. I had to quickly confront my fears or accept the consequences. I walked into the bathroom. I turned off the light and approached him placing my index finger on his lips as he was about to speak. I accepted the offer of his hand to help me join him in the shower. Initially, I stood behind him as he faced the spray of the showerhead, to hide my scars. I took the soap and used my hands to slowly wash his limbs, chest and erect penis.

I whispered, "Adam, I ran from you because I am afraid. I have never been with a man before and I feared the pain. Please be patient. I really do care for you and I want nothing more than to make love with you tonight."

His grin grew wider. He took the bar of soap from me and took his turn washing my wet body. Slowly, his hands caressed my inner thighs. I closed my eyes, enjoying the sensation of his touch. He massaged my breasts and between my legs. Our wet bodies locked in an embrace as our hands explored the contours of each other's body. I was so turned on by him that he became an obsession.

Adam turned off the water as his lips and tongue sensuously touched my lips, neck and breasts with wet kisses. We dried off while kissing each other.

"Adam, give me a minute and wait for me in my bed." The experience of wet foreplay was exhilarating and better than I could have ever imagined. I knew that this was the right man and I knew it was the right time. I had a tube of K-Y lubricant in the bathroom drawer. I dabbed it inside my vagina. In spite of my anxiety, I knew just what to do.

I found Adam laying on the bed. Using my mouth, I resurrected his penis and, after a couple of minutes before he exploded, I climbed on top of him. I lowered myself slowly working him into me one inch at a time. Eventually, I was a cowgirl on a bucking bronco. When penetration became too painful, I stopped, allowed my body to relax, and began moving my body up and down, front and back. I could tell that he enjoyed it by his groans of pleasure.

I didn't enjoy the act itself. I did enjoy pleasing him. I loved the smile on his face as he climaxed. God help me, I fell in love. A fearful thought crossed my mind. "Will he discard me when he learns I can't have children? Regardless, I will see if it can last before I worry."

Afterwards, we lay close, hugging one another. Our bodies were puzzle pieces that fitted perfectly in place. I could lay naked with this man forever. His body felt so comforting. Even the discomfort didn't seem to matter; it was a price I was willing to pay. I hoped that in time it would be less painful.

Adam brushed my hair back and said, "Making love with you tonight was special. I must confess you are the first girl I wanted a relationship with and didn't rush to have sex."

"You probably tell all the girls the same thing," I teased.

He pulled me close. "Hey, I try to share my heartfelt, honest feelings and you destroy the mood. You are such an asshole." By the grin on his face, I knew he was kidding.

"I'm glad you took your time with me. Being in bed with you tonight is emotionally fulfilling. I could never have imagined having a better lover than you. If I told you this earlier, I would have cried, and both of your heads would have swelled up and exploded." He laughed.

As he held me, he looked perplexed. He pointed to my scars and hesitantly asked, "They look like gunshot wounds?"

Embarrassed, I sat up, and hid my body under the blanket. He encouraged me to talk, and I knew I had to tell him. "I am going to share with you a secret that only my family knows. Remember, I told you that I was in London and Europe?"

"Yes?"

"There was a terrorist attack and I was one of the victims. The shrapnel ripped through my body. A girlfriend was killed. Time doesn't heal all wounds. There are days when I think about her and the life she could have lived. Some nights, I still have nightmares, as I recall those events. The days recuperating in the hospital were hard and painful."

Adam sat up and put his arms around me as he digested what I had shared with him. "Oh, my God. This was shortly after your parents died. I can't image how much pain you were in after those two horrific events. How long were you hospitalized?"

"It happened six months after my parents died. I was really fucked up for a while mentally. My friend, Gabrielle, and I had just become friends. After the bomb exploded, she searched for me and found me in the hospital. She too had wounds. The physical ones were minor compared to the mental trauma.

"Gabrielle made sure that I received the best medical care. Afterwards, I needed psychological therapy. She took me to a psychological treatment center in Europe. There they treated my emotional and psychological scars. That's where I learned French and my cooking skills. Without Gabrielle, who knows where I would be today. She literally saved my life."

The next morning, Adam went back to the frat house for a change of clothes. While he was gone, I called Gabrielle, yelling into the phone, "I am no longer a virgin! I did it. We had sex."

Gabrielle laughed with joy. She was excited for me. "You are a worry wart. How was it?"

I giggled before I told her. "It hurt like hell, but I followed your advice. I stopped whenever the pain was too intense so my body could relax. I enjoyed being close to him. I am going to be sore for the next day or two, but I want to do it again. I love making him happy. I think I love him. No, I *know* I love him, very much!"

Gabrielle said, "So, this is Adam in your class. The one you've been telling me about. I am so happy to hear that you found happiness and hopefully he'll be your soulmate."

"I told him how you nursed me back to health after I was injured. I told him that we lost our friend. Speaking of happiness, how are things going with you and Jack?"

Suddenly, I heard a knock on the door.

I said, "Shit, I think I hear Adam. He must be back from his frat house already. Gotta go, love you. We'll talk soon."

Sex or no sex, I was a taskmaster during the workday. I was relentless, making sure we were on schedule to solve the school assignment by the imposed deadline. During the day, my body wanted to cuddle and draw Adam close, but instead, I made him concentrate on work eight hours a day. I would rather be in the bedroom instead of on the computer as I saw the fruit of our labors coming together. We were close to a possible solution.

At night, the taskmaster became his love slave. I gave him all the love and affection a man could want.

After a few days, I rang Gabrielle. I said, "I'm sorry that I have not called you. I have to tell you everything. I was so sore Saturday. I could barely walk. Is there some Jewish law where you must have sex twice on Friday nights?"

She laughed. "There is a Jewish tradition for married couples to have sex on Friday night. Why do you ask? What did Adam tell you?"

"Well, he left out the married part. He is out right now, picking up dinner. I plan to surprise him when he returns."

"How?"

"I am wearing one of his button-down shirts, and nothing else."

Gabrielle gave a devilish chuckle. "Sounds like you have completely fallen for him. Keep in touch. I wonder how Jack would react if I surprised him the same way tonight?"

"Only one way to find out, girl! Do it, and let's compare notes tomorrow."

Adam used my key to let himself into the apartment. "Marci, I've got dinner," he called out.

I slowly opened my bedroom door and stood there with my legs spread, staring at him with my index finger saying 'come here'. Adam put the food on the table and rushed into the bedroom picking me and carrying me to the bed. Dinner was cold by the time we were ready to eat. In bed, I told him, "Davi is moving out of the apartment. Would you consider living with me?" He answered with a kiss.

We completed and submitted the project to our professor via email right before the deadline. We hoped that our answer was the correct solution. For six months we heard nothing. Then the dean of the engineering school summoned us to his office. In the room was our professor who introduced us to the two representatives from the Boeing Corporation. The older of the two Boeing employees looked at Adam and me with a warm grin before he spoke.

"Since last year, Boeing has sought a solution to a problem. Like many other companies, we offered a financial incentive to any university or independent thinker who could solve our technical issues. We required a solution for a software problem. We needed to increase our capacity to refuel multiple aircraft with tankers, midair, with minimal fuel loss in a time-efficient manner. We've tested your software program in actual military conditions."

Adam and I glanced at each other. We realized at this moment that we had properly analyzed the problem.

The representative said, "The program that you developed is exactly what we sought. Your solution will help our country's Air Force and Boeing. To compensate you for the software program you devised, my colleague and I are here to present you with this check in the amount of five hundred thousand dollars. Boeing has also donated an equal sum to your university's scholarship fund, in your names. Boeing would like to extend an offer of full-time employment to both of you upon graduation. If you accept our offer, you will have the option of working in our Chicago or Seattle headquarters."

We could hardly believe it! I was in shock. After thanking the Boeing reps, we left the office. In the hallway, I jumped in the air and landed in Adam's arms. I kissed him again and again. I only separated my lips from his long enough to say, "Wow, a year from now, we will both have our dream jobs!"

Adam, half-jokingly, said, "After taxes, this will make a great down payment on our first home."

He shocked me. Obviously, he had been secretly contemplating a lifetime commitment. I wanted to tell him that I wanted this relationship to be my first and my last. I was afraid so I said, "It is a great way to start a life together. Saving the money for our first home makes sense to me too."

The remaining months of senior year passed quickly.

Occasionally, on Friday nights, Beth, Ariel and their significant others came for dinner. During one of our evening get-togethers, Ariel said, "Marci, do you remember how I told you several times that I wanted to introduce you to a guy?"

I was unsure why she was bringing this up now so, I responded cautiously. "Yes?"

She smirked, "That guy was Adam. He told me that he wanted to go out with you the first time he saw you in class."

I looked at Adam. He nodded his head with a stupid grin. Then, we all had a good laugh. It was serendipitous that we had met and fallen in love all on our own.

Adam and I graduated. We took a month off and visited Europe and spent a few days in Cleveland with my family. Soon after that, we began our careers at the Boeing complex in Chicago. We worked on different floors for different corporate divisions. The month we began working was also the time we closed on our first home. It was a two-bedroom condominium downtown, facing Lake Michigan. We were within walking distance of the Magnificent Mile and Chicago's finest restaurants with a breathtaking view from our twenty-third-floor windows.

We fell into a comfortable domestic routine. We both shared in the chores and life was harmonious. We decided to keep a kosher home. I felt like an old married lady and was quite content. Thankfully, sex became pain-free, as we experimented with many different positions.

I loved living downtown, which was the perfect place for young lovers without children. There was always something happening: street fairs, bands, and theater. On evenings when we didn't work late, we frequented one of the many wonderful restaurants in walking distance from our place. When the weather cooperated with us, we walked home or walked over to the East Bank Club which was a premier fitness club in the city. The club was so close to work, I was able to take spinning and yoga classes during the week. Who could ask for a better life?

At bedtime, Adam held me while we engaged in pillow talk. We always kissed each other goodnight. However, something was bothering me, and I needed to pick the time and place to discuss it. One evening, I leaned over to him. I wanted to address my greatest fear, knowing it could end our love affair. His head was on his pillow and he was totally relaxed.

I said, "I have a pressing issue to discuss with you."

His immediate response was, "Are you pregnant?"

I barked at him, "Why would you even ask that?"

"I have never seen you take birth control, so I assumed that eventually it might happen."

I got angry and then apologetic. "I would never intentionally get pregnant without discussing it with you first. I am not that kind of girl. But since we are on that subject, I think you should know something."

His face grew concerned. He sat up. "What is it?"

Tears leaked from my eyes as I developed the courage to speak. "I can't have children."

Silently, Adam digested my words. Then, he said, "You scared me. You had been acting quiet and strange for the last couple of weeks. I feared you had a problem with me. I was wondering if you were going to tell me that you were pregnant or leave me. I love you. I want children and a family, but we can always adopt. Don't worry sweetheart, everything will work out for the best."

I hugged him and cried with relief. He could not get me to stop crying. I said, "You will never know how scared I was to tell you. I never want to lose you. I love you. As for children, we can find a surrogate. I too, want children and I want to give you a wonderful home."

Adam soothed me. "It's all going to be fine. Please go to sleep. We'll talk more tomorrow. I have to be at the office early in the morning."

"I can't go to sleep now. You made me so happy. I am so lucky to have you." Teary-eyed, I decided that I would give him a pleasure that I rarely performed for him. I pulled down the sheet and cover. I knew he was in heaven by the grunts, groans and the deep breaths that came from his mouth. His body tightened with pleasure, then relaxed as he achieved satisfaction. By the time I came back from the bathroom, he'd fallen asleep.

I tried to sleep, but my mind dwelled on our conversation. Adam had never asked why I couldn't have children. I could only assume that he surmised that it was a result of the injuries I suffered in London.

After three years of working at Boeing and logging overtime hours every week, I was getting tired of working these crazy hours. For what? I had money, but at this point, I wanted to get married, have children and a house in the suburbs. I brought the idea to Adam and he said, "Soon, just not yet."

Chapter 31

I willingly assumed the holiday cooking duties for my family in Cleveland. Now that Gabrielle was living there, we shared in the work. In recent years, Adam had joined me in Cleveland. Today, instead of calling Jack to tell him when we would arrive for the Jewish New Year, I had to tell him something else. I hoped he wouldn't be angry.

"Jack, how are you?"

"Good, and you? When are you guys coming in? We miss you."

"That's the reason for my call. We really want to be in Cleveland with all of you, but Adam's parents invited us to spend the holiday with them. As you know, my relationship with his mom is rocky. This is the first time she has invited the two of us. I feel guilty because I owe it to Adam, for the sake of his relationship with his parents. I hope you'll forgive me. You know I'd rather be there with you."

Jack laughed. "We love celebrating the holidays with our entire family, but I understand that sometimes we must share you. Tell Adam we love him. Hopefully, you will join us in spring for Passover and spend as many days with us as possible. We have a lot of catching up to do. We both miss you."

I said, "I can't wait. Maybe we'll meet you guys somewhere over the winter holidays."

Jack said, "By the way, I have a little gossip. Rumor has it that your friend, Ariel, and Brian might be announcing their engagement next month. It will be a sweet New Year. Maybe a family vacation is warranted."

"How exciting! Maybe I will fly in for the weekend. Are there any other engagement updates on the horizon that I should be penciling into my calendar? I thought maybe you'd be asking Gabrielle for her hand, too."

Jack chuckled. "You never know. If there is a date, Gabrielle will call you three seconds after I ask her. The two of you talk more than I thought was possible. Lucky for us, we're on the family plan, so your calls and texts do not count against our data package."

"I'll talk to you soon. Have a sweet and healthy New Year."

Jack said, "You too. Call us after the holiday. We want to know how dinner went at Adam's parents' home. You never know; maybe his mom wants to be your best friend."

I laughed as we disconnected.

Adam's parents, Greg and Barbara seldom visited us. In the beginning, his mother invited only Adam to family dinners, holiday celebrations, and special occasions. They pretended I didn't exist. When Adam asked for me to be included, his mom told him they were planning to discuss family business and it would be inappropriate.

In those days, Adam couldn't say no. He apologetically asked me for permission to see his family and I replied that I didn't mind being excluded, which was a lie.

His mother preferred Adam's high school sweetheart who lived next door over me. His mom made sure the ex was there when I wasn't. I finally told Adam, "If they do not want me to attend the dinner, I am not going somewhere that I'm not invited. So, excuse me, but screw them. I do not know why your mother does not like me. That's her problem, not mine. But if we want to be a family then we should attend family functions together, or not at all!"

After two years together, I was finally invited as a guest at their family's Sunday night dinner. However, his mother didn't speak to me during the entire evening and I wished I hadn't come. "Adam, I will never allow your mom to treat me in such a fashion again. I'm pissed, because you didn't stand up for me either."

After that night, Adam told his parents that either I was to be treated like a member of the family or he would no longer come over for holidays or family dinners. His mother was shocked and his father quietly disappointed when Adam stopped showing up. That was three years ago when we had just started our jobs.

So, I was surprised when, out of the blue, his mother invited us for Rosh Hashanah. Barbara personally called and invited me. She even remembered my name this time. Maybe a miracle happened, and his mother decided to start the New Year on a positive note.

I jokingly remarked, "I had better check my food for arsenic."

"She wouldn't do that," Adam said, but I noticed he looked nervous. I guess he was worried whether his mom would poison me.

All I knew was that we were going to Adam's parents' house for dinner and then we were to join them for services at their synagogue. I was dressed for the occasion. I wore my new black, Oscar de la Renta suit and a pink silk blouse, my mother's diamond pendant, and the diamond stud earrings Gabrielle and Cristina had given me.

On the way to his parent's home, we stopped and purchased a bouquet of flowers and a good bottle of kosher red wine. We drove up the long driveway to the circular turn-around in front of their huge house. It was a beautiful, century-old residence, built with brown stone. My childhood home could have fit inside their great room.

Everything was festive and we were warmly welcomed. The dining room table was formally set with three forks, three spoons and two knives at each place setting. The plates were exquisite: Royal Doulton English Porcelain. I was impressed. Tonight, only the immediate family was invited. There were five of us, including Adam's brother, Seth.

We presented the wine and flowers to his mother upon our arrival. Mrs Cohen, as she preferred to be called, was there to greet us. Adam's dad was standing behind her. Lack of exercise and poor eating habits had left Mr Cohen, Greg, with a Winston Churchill physique. Yet, he had a salesman's gift of humor and the ability to maintain a conversation with anyone.

Mrs Cohen wore a striking royal blue dress with matching jacket. She had perspiration on her forehead from cooking dinner.

"Happy New Year, Mrs Cohen," I said.

She kissed me on the cheek and pleasantly responded, "Please call me Barbara or Barb, whichever you prefer."

I was taken aback by her friendliness. I wanted to make a good impression, so I asked, "May I help you in the kitchen?"

"There is nothing to do, but if you want to keep me company, that would be lovely."

Barbara handed me an apron to protect my outfit. Our conversation started slowly as we discussed the weather and work. I complimented her, saying, "Your holiday decorations are lovely and the food smells delicious."

She asked me questions about my family. She wanted to know everything there was to know about me now, but I was being careful not to disclose too much. I answered her questions only sharing what I wanted her to know without sounding evasive.

I felt very uncomfortable telling a virtual stranger all the hardships I endured. To change subjects, I often asked her questions. After fifteen minutes she didn't learn much. Then, she tried another approach, eliciting answers with charm.

"Adam tells me that you enjoy cooking. Did your mother teach you how to cook?"

I thought for a second and crafted a response that would satisfy her. "My parents died when I was still in high school. They were killed by a drunk truck driver. After high school, I traveled to Europe for a year where I worked as the assistant to a French chef at a spa. In college, I volunteered to help out in the kitchen at the Chabad House. I find cooking is relaxing and gives me inner peace. Now, I only cook for Adam or family in Cleveland when I spend the holidays with them."

Barbara paused, taking this in. Without looking at me she said, "My son loves you very much, and I want him to be happy." I had no idea why she said that. I was expecting her to say, "Sorry for your loss."

Adopting the same tone, I replied, "I love your son. He is my heart and my reason for being. I want to make him happy forever."

Barbara smiled at me and I sensed the slightest bit of softening. She asked me to join her as we lit the holiday candles to usher in the Jewish New Year. Afterwards, she gave me a warm and affectionate embrace. She whispered in my ear, "May God bless you with a wonderful New Year."

We had just eaten apples and honey, and everyone was engaged in friendly conversations when Adam stood up with a glass in his hand. He cleared his throat and lightly tapped his crystal wine glass with his spoon.

"I have an announcement."

Magically, everyone stopped talking and looked at him.

He said, "I love you, Marci."

I did not want to be the center of attention and motioned for him to sit down but he continued. "I called Jack last week and he gave me permission to ask you for your hand in marriage. So, I will not sit down until you agree to become my wife." In the palm of his hand lay a beautiful engagement ring.

The moment was so surreal, I screamed with joy.

"I can't believe it. I love you!" I said. I stood next to him in shock, weeping.

"Is that a yes?" he asked.

"Yes, Yes, I will now, and forever be your wife." I jumped into his arms. Adam, Seth and Greg laughed, but I could not stop my tears from flowing. He placed the ring on my finger.

Barbara came around the table toward me. She said, "Welcome to the family, Marci. I wish, in time that you will feel comfortable enough to call me 'Mom'."

I sensed a friendly truce.

Adam winked at me. He said, "Next weekend, we will go and pick out the wedding ring."

I silently answered him with a nod. I could not find words to speak. After such a shock and wonderful surprise, I lost my appetite. I had so much on my mind that I didn't want to eat. However, how could I do that to Barb after she'd spent hours cooking? The meal was delicious. She was an accomplished cook.

I was impatient and couldn't wait to ask Adam a slew of questions as we got into the car on the way to services. "How long ago did you decide to ask me? So, who else knew? When I called Cleveland last week, did they already know?"

Adam confessed. "I wanted to marry you from the moment we started dating. I am sorry that I did not ask you sooner. To steal your phrase: you make me a more complete person. Yes, everyone knew, including Jack and Gabrielle."

We returned home and my first phone call was to Jack and Gabrielle. We talked for over an hour. Gabrielle wanted to hear every detail.

I said, "I was shocked when he asked me. I couldn't stop crying. Adam stood up and formally asked me to be his bride. It was so romantic."

After the holiday, I called Fiora to share my good news. Then I called Beth, Davi and Ariel. I asked each of them to be in my bridal party. I also phoned Hilda and Shosh and told them that I hoped they would attend the wedding, even though we hadn't picked a date.

Two weeks later, I arranged to meet Barbara for lunch. I chose to meet her at Gibson's on Rush Street. It was a swanky restaurant with outrageously good food. I started the conversation slowly, but words rushed out of my mouth, since I had so much to say.

"Barbara, thank you for meeting with me today. I thought it would be a good idea for just us girls to discuss wedding plans."

I could tell from her defensive body language she was somewhat guarded, as I spoke.

"Adam and I are considering a wedding in late August or September. I want to ask you a favor. Would you help me pick out my wedding dress? Do you think it would be too early to start shopping next week? I am clueless. I do not know where to shop for wedding dresses or where to find a wedding planner. Would you be willing to help me?"

Barb smiled and looked pleased. She even looked a little choked up.

I continued. "This is so new to me. I have never hosted a large catered event, let alone one that holds so much importance for me. I was thinking of hiring a professional, but I don't know anyone, nor the questions that I should be asking. I know it's a lot of work and if you say no or that you don't have the time, I understand, but I am lost, and I need your help."

Barbara affectionately looked at me, reached across the table, and patted my hand. "I am honored that you asked me. I would love to assist you, but under one condition; it's your wedding, not mine. If you don't like my suggestions, you can be honest and tell me. I will harbor no ill will. Agreed?" I agreed.

"Have you and Adam discussed what type of wedding or ceremony you want? Have you discussed how many guests you'll invite or the type of venue you prefer? Have you thought about a date or a time of the year?"

I shook my head and laughed. "Last night, he wanted to have the ceremony at Wrigley Field. He wanted the wedding party to come out of the third base dugout wearing Cubs' jerseys, with our names embroidered on the back."

Barbara shook her head and asked, "What do you want?"

Every girl dreams of their wedding day. I was no different. I said, "I would like the wedding on September 8, the anniversary of our first date. I would love an outdoor wedding ceremony with nature as our backdrop. The venue must have the last-minute option to accommodate an indoor ceremony depending on the weather."

I noticed the wrinkles on her face turn to a smile as I talked. "I want to be married in a traditional Jewish ceremony with a rabbi, under the chuppah. The religious aspects of the ceremony are important to me. I want the meal and the dancing inside so bugs or any threats of the weather will not ruin it."

Barbara said, "The most important thing you need to do is to reserve your room and a caterer as soon as possible. Everything else, we have time to plan for."

"My family is small and, combined with Adam and our friends, we wouldn't have more than one hundred guests. How many people would your side of the family want to invite?"

"We have a larger group, between one hundred and one hundred and twenty-five guests. If there is a question of finances, we would be glad to help with the cost."

"Traditionally, I believe the groom's family sponsors the dinner before the wedding and the liquor bill. I have money set aside to cover the rest."

We chose a few dates to look for wedding dresses. She insisted on picking up the check for lunch and I let her treat me. Afterwards, she hugged me.

"You made me very happy today," she said.

My eyes began to water. "I know how much my mother would have wanted to be here. I hope that we can continue to be closer than just friends. Thank you for a marvelous lunch."

Barb wasted no time. The next week, she had come up with several locations to visit. She secured the name of a highly recommended wedding planner who would be a good fit for what we envisioned.

Months passed and between work and the wedding, I felt life closing in on me. I flew to Cleveland for a badly needed break. Gabrielle and Jack met me at the airport. I shared my stress and how I was overwhelmed as the wedding date approached. I figured a couple of days at my Cleveland home would give me a much-needed opportunity to clear my mind and relax.

Gabrielle already knew that she was going to be my maid of honor, so I formally asked Jack to give me away and walk me down the aisle. Jack accepted, as I knew he would.

We were out for dinner during my visit, when I noticed a jewelry box in Jack's hand. "Marci, Gabrielle and I wanted to give you something special from us in honor of your wedding. This is a keepsake that we hope you will always cherish and wear on special occasions. Gabrielle gets all the credit for selecting it."

Like a child, I quickly unwrapped the gift. I stared at it, speechless. Inside the black velvet box was a pair of diamond and blue sapphire dangling earrings.

I gasped. "Stunning! Exquisite! I have never ever seen anything so beautiful. You shouldn't have."

"We should have, and we did," Gabrielle said.

I asked, "Would you help me try them on? I can't wait to see how they look."

Jack said, "It's an English custom that brides wear something old, something new, something borrowed and something blue on their wedding day. If you wear your mom's diamond pendant, these earrings, and a gold ankle chain that Gabrielle will lend you, then you will be covered."

We hugged. I cried and thanked them both. "Jack, when did you become an expert on English wedding traditions? Have you and Gabrielle been planning?" They looked at one another and then smiled.

The pre-wedding events began. My three college roommates suggested that we meet in New York City to celebrate, the weekend before the wedding. I called Fiora, Gabrielle, Hilda and Barbara to invite them as well.

The backstory of the bachelorette trip was more eventful than the trip itself. Barbara and I talked on the flight and I told her all about the other women attending my wedding party. Upon arriving at the hotel and meeting everyone, Barbara immediately asked to share a room with Hilda. I was a little nervous because 'Nancy Drew' could be tough with her questions. I worried that perhaps Barbara thought she could learn nuggets about my past from Hilda in the privacy of their hotel room.

Assertively, Gabrielle spoke up, "I am rooming with you, sister."

When we got to our room, I asked, "Why were you so pushy, demanding to be my roommate in the way you did?"

"I was afraid that you would have roomed with Fiora."

"So what? I love Fiora and I always will. She was my first love. I love Adam and I would not throw away a lifetime with him for an evening of sex."

"I know you wouldn't, but I saw the way the two of you embraced when you saw her in the hotel lobby. I know the control Fiora can have over you and how tempting she could be."

"I know you are always watching out for me. That's why I love you so much. Now, get dressed. We have an evening of partying."

Barbara approached me on the following day. "I'm having so much fun. Thank you for treating me like one of the girls. Very few mothers-in-law are invited to the bachelorette party. You really made me feel special."

"You're welcome, Barb. I am glad you decided to join us. It means a lot to me that you are here. I think we will all have a good time."

She said, "I overheard your conversation with your friend yesterday in the lobby. I think her name is Fiora? I only took two years of French twenty years ago, so I barely understood two words of what you two were saying. I never realized that you are so fluent. Does she speak English?"

I chose my words carefully. "Fiora now lives in Israel. French is her native tongue. She speaks English, however, it may be a little rusty. She taught me French and I helped her with math homework. Would you like me to properly introduce you? I think you will find her a very engaging woman. At one time, she was my closest friend."

The first night, we returned to the hotel a little hungover, four hours before sunrise. Gabrielle and I barely got out of our clothes before our heads hit our pillows. It had been difficult to find the time to talk, with our packed itinerary.

Before she fell asleep, Gabrielle mumbled, "Jack and I decided to put off our engagement until after you, Adam, Ariel and Brian get married. We did not want to impose on our children's celebrations."

I told her that was not necessary, but Jack and Gabrielle had already made up their minds. We quickly drifted off to sleep.

It was time to leave New York. We said our goodbyes and headed in separate directions. Barb and I slept on the flight. When we landed, we called for a limo to take us to Barbara's home. Barb had planned a catered dinner party for that evening. We had a couple of hours to shower and change before the guests were scheduled to arrive. Members of Adam's extended family and closest friends were invited to meet and greet the bride. I was not looking forward to this evening, because I was not the type of person who enjoyed basking in the limelight. However, it was one obligation I could not ignore.

I got through it and, at the end of the evening, I hugged Barbara. I said, "You have been like a mother to me. There is no way for me to properly thank you for your work and the countless hours you've put in. Thank you for making sure every wedding detail is perfect. I am fortunate to have you."

Our wedding was not at Wrigley Field. It was held at Beth El Synagogue in Highland Park. Lake Michigan, in all its splendor, was the backdrop for the ceremony. Guests faced the powder blue waters as seagulls flew overhead against the blue sky. During the ceremony, the guests watched a flotilla of sailboats with colorful sails glide across the lake.

Our wedding canopy was made of white embroidered cloth. Fresh blue and purple flowers were sewn into the fabric, along with blessings for love and happiness. The four posts of the canopy were wrapped with ivy, as a salute to Wrigley Field and the Cubs.

The weather was perfect. Everyone had a wonderful time. I think my parents would have been proud of us. As I symbolically circled Adam seven times, forever combining our souls as one, I counted my blessings. I would forever remember this day!

Chapter 32

By the time I turned twenty-nine, I had been many different people; a son, girlfriend, and now a wife. My dreams and aspirations continued to evolve and change. I no longer wanted to be that 'Corporate Success Story'.

Adam and I had been married for four years and I wanted more out of life. I was jealous of Brian and Ariel, who had one child already and a second one on the way. They lived comfortably in a four-bedroom home in Beachwood, not far from Jack and Gabrielle. Brian, after paying his dues, became a partner in the law firm started by Jack and my dad. Ariel authored a 'What's Happening in Cleveland' column for the *Cleveland Plain Dealer*. She also wrote a news blog. I don't know how she handled all her family and job responsibilities. I wanted what she had.

Fiora got pregnant via artificial insemination and gave birth to a beautiful baby girl named Jordona. Her Israeli soldier became a CPA after they both left the army. I met Fiora's heartthrob nine months after the wedding when we vacationed in Israel. Fiora truly lucked out. The two of them looked so beautiful in their white wedding dresses.

It was an easy time for the people I knew. Brett, Jack's second son, was planning his wedding. Gabrielle and Jack were enjoying life; traveling and spending time with their grandchildren. The Chabad rabbi who helped us during Helen's last Passover, officiated at both Gabrielle's conversion and the wedding ceremony.

Beth had two kids and Davi fulfilled her dream of working for Google in California. Davi was busy, happy, unmarried, and always dating some new, wonderful guy. Hilda employed two younger psychiatrists at the Compound and, in time, hoped to reduce her hours and semi-retire.

Meanwhile, I climbed up the rungs of the corporate ladder at Boeing. I was promoted to project manager in the aircraft design division. Perhaps they kept promoting me because I kept saying 'no' to being transferred overseas. Maybe no one ever told them that before, so they were trying to use reverse psychology on me. Who knows? I had been successful in handling whatever work they assigned me over the years. Management at Boeing acknowledged my collaboration with co-workers and graded me with the highest evaluations from my superiors. I worked overtime every week but, as a general rule, I was home to light candles and cook Sabbath dinner for Adam.

As happy as I was for everyone else, I was feeling some stress on the home front. For the last few months, Adam worked almost around the clock. I never knew if, or when, he would be home. I became despondent and frustrated by Adam's priorities. He had changed and become his workaholic father.

I finished the process of searching for a surrogate and house hunting in the suburbs near Barbara. Adam was no help. He couldn't pry himself from the office, even on a Sunday.

When Gabrielle called to check in, I grabbed my phone. She and Jack had just returned from their three-week honeymoon at a resort in the Amazon rainforest. "You are my first call," she said. "I missed you! There was no cell phone reception or Internet, but our honeymoon was amazing. I can't wait to tell you about it. What's happening with you guys?"

Like a race car, words flowed without pausing for a breath. "Girl, I'm at my wits end. I'm very grateful you called. Life is bittersweet. I told you that we found a beautiful young girl to be our surrogate. Her name is Erin. I am only ten years older and she sees me as a mother figure. Her insemination last week appears to have been successful, but we need to wait and see. I invited her to live with us so I can monitor her diet and exercise during the pregnancy."

"That's great news! Why don't I sense excitement in your voice?

I started out answering the easiest questions first. However, my words conveyed sadness. "I told you we were house hunting and I made an offer on one before you left. I loved it. After the inspectors checked it out, I went to the sellers and asked if I could have immediate occupancy if I agreed to pay cash."

"Did they agree?"

"They did. The house was empty. Right after you left, we closed. The day after the closing I had the house painted, cleaned, minor repairs completed, and we moved in. Coordinating the house repairs and moving has been hectic. Thankfully, Erin and Barb have been amazing. They took care of most of the details."

Gabrielle made sounds of approval. "Tell me about your home."

"It's not far from Adam's mother's new home. It's two levels with four bedrooms on a huge lot. Our future kids will love playing in the spacious backyard. There is a wonderful patio. We have a deck suitable for entertaining. The house is three blocks from a synagogue and public park, and only seven blocks from the train station. We have great neighbors. Several have already introduced themselves and offered us assistance. Many are professionals with young families, just like us."

"How do you like having Erin around?"

"She has been a great help to me around the house and I find her companionship wonderful and needed. She seems to enjoy living with us, even though the house is disorganized. The train allows her the freedom to travel to the city, so she hangs with her friends when she wants."

Gabrielle interrupted, "So, if everything is so great, why are you so glum? Talk to me. I know you. I can tell from your voice that something is upsetting you. With a new house and a child on the way, you should be crying with joy in your heart."

My words were muddled as tears gathered. "I am worried about Adam. I wonder if our marriage will survive."

Gabrielle demanded clarification. "Catch your breath and start from the beginning."

I explained. "Adam earned a promotion. He is now a project manager responsible for the construction of a new commercial jetliner. He has undertaken control of the scheduling and the manufacturing of this new type of aircraft. Boeing made deals with numerous countries including India, Vietnam, China and Bulgaria to guarantee the financial success of the project. As part of the sales agreement Boeing agreed to have components of this aircraft manufactured in those countries."

I took a breath and sipped on a bottle of water. "For instance, the wings can be made in China, the fuselage in India, and the landing gear in Vietnam. The problem is monitoring the quality and production timing. It is a thankless, endless job. Production problems caused the first project manager to retire early and the airplane's first flight has been delayed by one year because of manufacturing and software problems."

Gabrielle said, "Could you be overreacting? You aren't telling me why you think your marriage is on the rocks. It sounds like Adam is just putting in additional time at the office until your first baby arrives, so he can spend more time with you afterwards."

I said, "No. It's not like that at all. Adam has been obsessed with his responsibilities. In the last twelve weeks, he hasn't left work before ten p.m. Some nights, he never comes home. If I call him to ask where he is, he responds with a text message to say he is sleeping on his office couch or at a motel on Ohio street. We have not had a real conversation in weeks. He stopped telling me that he loves me, and we haven't had sex in three months. I was too embarrassed to tell you before your trip. Things are only getting worse. I am worried about him. I'm afraid he is headed for a nervous breakdown."

Gabrielle's tone was concerned. She said, "Ariel is expecting her second child in a week. Can you come to Cleveland this weekend, so we can spend time together before the baby arrives?"

I dabbed tears from my eyes. "Great idea. I have countless hours of unused vacation time. I will take a week off and come to see you. I desperately need to talk to you face to face. I need your wisdom. I am afraid that Adam has married his work and abandoned me, his wife. I would rather have Adam than the money. I don't need any more money and I don't know how to communicate my fears to him."

While I cried my heart out, Gabrielle suddenly gasped with exuberance. She said, "Forgive me, but Jack just walked in. Brian called from the hospital and their new baby boy will be joining the family any time now. We'll host his circumcision at our house in eight days."

My mood quickly changed. "How wonderful! I will make my flight arrangements as soon as we hang up. I can fly in early to help with the set-up and get your advice. I will text you my flight schedule later. I may stay for three or four days after the Bris. I am too sad to function right now. Maybe some family time will cheer me up."

"If you need me, call me!" Gabrielle was always the mother hen. "Don't do or say anything that you'll later regret to Adam. It's hard right now, but you both have been blessed. Think of those blessings, and you'll get through this tough stretch."

"See you soon! I'll call you with my flight. Send my love to Ariel, Brian and Jack."

I got off the phone, feeling depressed. I turned on my computer and booked my flight. Later that day, I told Erin that I was going out of town to attend a family celebration and would stay a few extra days to visit. Erin and I went shopping for a week's worth of food and I made sure to give her money in case she needed anything else. She had my cell phone number in the event of an emergency. I also gave her Gabrielle's numbers.

I did not tell Adam or leave him a note. If he didn't return home to sleep, he wouldn't notice that our bed was empty and cold. If he cared, he could call me.

Chapter 33

Adam's father, Greg, had suffered lower abdominal pains and experienced traces of blood in his urine for several months. When Greg finally told Barbara about his persistent condition, she exerted her will, made a doctor's appointment, and practically dragged him by the hand to the physician's office.

The first tests came back inconclusive. The doctors ordered additional tests at the University of Chicago medical facility. Those tests did not come back with favorable results. Greg and Barbara sat in a small office for over an hour waiting for the diagnosis. The wait was nerve-racking. Finally, the doctor walked into the room. He lowered his glasses and looked at the test results again, shaking his head.

His manner was professional, but unemotional. "Greg and Barbara, it appears Greg has an advanced stage of bladder and liver cancer. We suspect additional cancer cells may have populated in the surrounding organs. We will know more after we open him up and test some tissue samples. We will also perform a CT scan for the same purpose. Then, we will determine the best course of action."

A day passed, the doctors performed their tests and once again Greg and Barbra heard a less than hopeful prognosis.

Barbara looked at the doctor, demanding answers. "What are his chances of survival?" The doctor didn't look at her eyes when he shook his head.

She tried again, saying, "If Greg was your spouse or child, which hospital and which doctors would offer him the greatest chance of survival?"

"We have one of the finest oncology departments in the world, right here in Chicago." He paused as he digested her words. "However, with your husband's type of cancer, you might want to contact the Anderson Cancer Center in Houston. If you'd like, I can assist with arranging an appointment. I know several doctors there and, with your permission, I can forward my findings to them. If you give me twenty minutes, my assistant will make the arrangements and provide you with a doctor's name and appointment information."

Barb was shell-shocked. She looked over to Greg, who seemed to convey, "I'm leaving the decision in your hands."

Barbara responded. "Yes, please make the arrangements. Thank you."

As Greg and Barbara received this devastating news, I landed in Cleveland, walked to the pickup area and saw a sight for sore eyes; Gabrielle was at the curb waiting for me.

I said, "Girl, I've missed you. Thank you for picking me up."

"Get in the car, throw your bag in the back seat. Tell me all about Erin and the pregnancy." She wanted me to start talking about something positive before discussing the more pressing issues. It was a technique she learned at the Compound to disarm an angry patient.

"Yes, she missed her period and the home test indicates she's going to have our child."

"That's great news. Where did you find her?"

I said, "Well, she advertised on a website called GoFundMe. She offered to be a surrogate for a family who would be willing to underwrite her college education. I interviewed twenty other candidates, but I fell in love with her. Regardless, I checked her out. I made her take blood tests for drugs and diseases. I totally screened her. I learned that she was accepted to the University of Illinois but didn't have the money for tuition. I offered her the normal surrogate fee of twenty-five thousand dollars. Then, I sweetened the deal by agreeing to pay for her undergraduate education, including board and books, after the child is born. I told her she could live with us to save money during the pregnancy and for the first few months afterwards while she recovers. I would cover all her medical expenses. We went to an attorney and had a contract drafted for everyone's protection."

"Sounds like everybody wins," Gabrielle said.

I nodded and said, "I also negotiated a second contract with her. If she decides to have a second child for us, I will pay her another seventy-five thousand dollars. I figured that would be a win-win. Erin gets an education that could lead to a career and we'd have two children with the same DNA."

Gabrielle looked at me and, by her expression, I knew it was time for the subject to change. "It sounds like you're in a good place with Erin and the child. Now, tell me about Adam."

We pulled into a Starbucks. I waited to bear my soul until after we had ordered our lattes. With drinks in hand, we walked over to the patio area. I took a sip and then began to spill my guts. "Four months ago, Adam started this project at work. As I told you on the phone, it's been a disaster from day one. After a year of failures, the project keeps getting worse. Adam has put his life into this assignment, working seven days a week. He has totally abandoned me. I'm feeling alone and unwanted. He doesn't even return my texts or emails."

Gabrielle paused and, with trepidation, asked, "Forgive me, don't hate me for asking, but could he be having an affair?"

She threw me for a loop. It was a possibility that I had not considered. I hesitated before answering. "I don't think so. I think it's the job. I hope it's not an affair. I believe he is overwhelmed and stressed out."

"I had to ask," Gabrielle said.

I got angry after thinking about her question again. "If it's an affair, I'll kill him. If it's his job, I am afraid he will kill himself. His work will destroy our marriage and his health."

"How long will this project last?"

"At least another two years, maybe longer." Gabrielle paused to choose her words carefully. "Can you talk to his mother? If not, maybe you need to confront him in the office, where he can't escape you. I know it can be messy having it out at work, but you may have no choice at this point."

While Gabrielle and I were drinking, Barbara was calling Adam back in Chicago. "Adam? I need to talk to you."

"It's a bad time. Can we talk later?" Adam's second cell phone began to ring, in addition to his second work landline. "Mom, it's super crazy here today. I promise to call you later this week."

With that, Barbara was disconnected, which left her indignant. She shoved her phone back into her purse and composed herself. She drove Greg over to Manny's Deli, a Chicago institution. She stopped in front of the restaurant and told her husband to go inside and order his favorite pastrami sandwich. Manny's was Greg's best loved restaurant. Seldom did he allow himself the time to enjoy their famous deli cuisine. He was more than willing to sit down and relax with a hot pastrami sandwich on rye bread, garnished with mustard and a fresh pickle. He gave Barbara a kiss, and she promised to pick him up in an hour.

From Manny's, Barbara drove to Boeing's headquarters. She parked her car on Washington Boulevard, walked over the Chicago River Bridge, and entered the Boeing building. At the security desk, she showed her driver's license and asked for Adam's office. Adam's assistant came to escort her to his office. A long table strewn with used coffee cups, containers of food, diagrams and design software printouts sat in the middle of the room. Papers of every size and color littered the floor and were tossed haphazardly under the desks and chairs.

There were two chairs facing Adam's desk. Barbara sat down in one of them as the assistant closed the door. Adam was annoyed to see his mother.

In a rushed and unapologetic manner, he said, "Mom, I don't have time for this. Do you hear all the phones ringing? I am glad you are downtown, but this week is not the week to visit. You should have called for an appointment."

Barbara held up her hand and issued an order. "Do not pick up the telephone and do not say a word. I am your mother and I will not be treated like garbage. Your father has been diagnosed with cancer. I'm going to Houston to see specialists there."

Adam gaped at her in shock.

A strong woman, Barbara hid her tears while expressing the anger she felt for her son. "If your

273

brother was in town and not on some Asian river cruise, I would not even be bothering you. I thought you would want to come with me to Houston while your father gets a second opinion and they perform additional tests to confirm the diagnosis."

Adam looked down at his desk and said, "Mom, I am actually very busy. My job depends on this project. If the doctor finds something serious, I'll fly down, but for now, my hands are tied. I will have my secretary book flights for you and Dad, leaving tomorrow. I can get you a room in the best hotel. Dad is strong. He is not even sixty years old. He will be fine. The doctors are always scaring their patients for no reason except to make money. I don't think you have to worry."

Barbara could not believe Adam's reaction. She stood, gathered her things, and left before she said something that she would later regret. She held her emotions in check until she got into her car. Then, her dignity evaporated. She begged God for help. She pressed the starter button, collected herself and drove back to Manny's.

Greg had slobbered mustard on his shirt and cleaned his plate by the time Barbara returned. He really enjoyed the hot, thick, spicy sandwich, but his attention immediately switched from his pastrami to his wife's obvious distress. He tried to console her.

"Barbara, I feel too good to be dying. The shithead doctors screwed up. Nobody who feels as good as I do can be dying of cancer. The only reason I want to visit

Houston is because they have the best steak joints. I remember eating a sixteen-ounce prime rib steak. I really was sick that night, remember?"

He laughed, but Barbara refused to join in. She knew this was life-and-death and Greg was using humor to deflect the gravity of the diagnosis.

Back in Cleveland, I received a text message from Adam. He wrote: 'Dad is on the way to a hospital called MD Anderson in Houston. Don't know what's wrong. Can you help Mom? She seems out of sorts and wanted me to go, but too busy. Love you.'

If I'd had a baseball bat and was within striking distance of Adam, I would have knocked some sense into his thick skull. I Googled the name of the clinic and learned that it was a top cancer research and treatment center.

I looked up from my phone at Gabrielle. "Barbara is taking Greg to a cancer hospital in Houston tomorrow."

"You're joking."

"I'm absolutely serious. Adam just texted. No one is with them. Barbara needs my support. Please tell Jack and everyone I wish I could stay, but I need to be in Houston."

I booked the first available flight on my smartphone's browser. I was only in Cleveland for one night and didn't have time to see everyone. The new baby and his celebration would have to wait for another visit. Gabrielle drove me back to the airport the next morning, a little after sunrise.

I arrived in Houston and took a cab straight to the hospital, where I asked for Greg's room. I was directed to the lobby, where I found Barbara.

Weary-eyed, she looked at me in disbelief. "Marci, what are you doing here? How did you know where to find me?"

I reached for Barbara's hand and tried to comfort her. "I got a text from Adam."

She clutched my arm and said, "Thank you for coming. The doctors are reviewing Greg's medical records and examining him in the adjacent room. The doctors in Chicago didn't believe that Greg's chances are good. They weren't sure how much the cancer spread."

She took deep breaths and bit her lip to prevent herself from completely breaking down. I put my arm around her and pulled her close.

When she was composed, Barbara focused at me and said, "Your husband is not the son I remember. He was a good and respectful child. I tried calling him and he wouldn't return my calls or texts. I drove to see him at work. He offered to make the plane and hotel reservations, but then he threw me out of his office like a beggar. 'Here are a couple of dollars, now leave.' I was mortified. If you don't mind my asking, is he like this at home?"

I was emotionally drained and didn't want to get started by venting my feelings about Adam. "All I can say now is that Adam is extremely stressed at work. He is not his normal self. He's working seven days a week and I have not seen much of him in months." I started to get upset, took a deep breath, and sighed. "Let's talk about your son later, please."

Barbara shook her head, disappointed in the son she raised. We sat in the waiting room, each deep in our own thoughts. A nurse approached us. "Are you here for Greg Cohen? Please follow me."

We walked down the cold, sterile hospital halls to the doctors' conference room. We took seats at the table. Already seated were two doctors, and one hospitalist. Greg sat in a wheelchair.

"Please sit down, Mrs Cohen."

"Doctor, this is my daughter-in-law, Marci."

On the wall, a monitor the size of a large flat screen television displayed images of Greg's lungs, bladder and liver. "Do you see these circled areas? Those are areas of cancer concentration. We believe this may be the extent of the problem, but we cannot be sure until we operate and remove this mass here." His laser pen highlighted the areas. The cancer is aggressive and spreading. Our recommended plan would be to surgically remove the affected areas and treat him with concentrated chemotherapy."

The surgeon paused to allow his words to sink in. Barbara covered her mouth with her hands. She was shaking.

"What are our other options?" I asked.

The doctor said, "We can try experimental drugs. You can return to your home and allow Greg to live his remaining days without any further treatments. Or, we can operate, but there are dangers. We will need to locate a liver transplant donor if we proceed with surgery. We can see if you have a compatible family member; otherwise, we will need to seek one from the donor list."

Barbara reached for Greg's hand and asked, "Are you saying surgery is the best choice?"

The doctor interrupted. "Not necessarily. Because of Greg's weight and high blood pressure, there are added risks associated with surgery."

It was a lot of information to take in. I grabbed Barbara's other hand as she listened to the doctor's words. She squeezed my hand harder, yet she continued to shake.

"How long will he live if he goes home now, without any treatments?"

"It's tough to say. Maybe three months." Out of the corner of my eye, I saw Greg's hand cover his mouth.

Barbara's voice became frantic. She asked, "What success have you had with medications alone to achieve a remission?"

"Limited success. In your husband's case, the side effects could cause his death."

Greg said, "So the pills that are supposed to save my life would kill me? It sounds like I'm better off drinking gasoline."

The doctor said, "To answer your question more directly, we have not had success with the experimental medications with his stage of cancer."

"With surgery, what are his chances?"

"Again, your husband is overweight, with high blood pressure. Fifty-fifty, at best, if he survives the operation. But there is only a fifty-fifty chance we can eradicate most of the cancer without chemo. Chemo has inherent risks, too. There is a fifty-fifty chance the treatments will result in a remission of the remaining cancer cells and stop the growth of new cells."

I calculated the probability for a positive outcome and knew they were not good. Greg had a twelve per cent chance of long-term survival. I didn't like those odds.

Barbara peered at Greg. Words were conveyed with their eyes. "Please schedule the surgery. In the meantime, let me talk to Greg privately. We will discuss the other options you offered."

I found myself admiring her composure. I truly do not know if I could have handled this decision as well as she did.

Greg signed the surgical permission forms and was checked into the hospital. That night, Barbara slept in her clothes on the recliner next to Greg's bed. I wanted to stay too, but she insisted that I return to their hotel and spend the evening there. I slept in Barbara's bed at the hotel and gathered the personal items she would need in the morning.

I returned to the hospital at five a.m., an hour before the scheduled surgery. I sat with Barbara until Greg was wheeled into the operating room. He was in good spirits. With a smile, he said, "Don't worry, I'll be fine."

We were asked to stay in the family waiting room down the hall. Except for washroom breaks and numerous cups of coffee, we sat there for more than five hours. I muted the large television screen and tried to pass the time consoling Barb.

She was reliving earlier days, when her children were young, and life was less complicated. "Adam was my favorite. Every morning he would run to me in his pajamas to hug me. Now, I don't recognize him."

We reminisced about my wedding and the years since then. She continued to talk. At one point she asked, "Marci, do you think I like my house?"

I was not sure what to say, but said, "Your house is truly beautiful.

She laughed and said, "I hate it. What do I need such a large house for? I grew up in a two-story walk-up in West Rogers Park, a working-class neighborhood. I attended Boone, a public school and Mather High School. Greg wanted to show off his success to his friends and colleagues. I wanted to be the perfect wife, so I went along with his charade. I would have wanted a house like the house you and Adam have."

My mother-in-law abruptly changed the subject and asked how Jack and Gabrielle were doing. I told her they had recently become grandparents for the second time and Jack's youngest was getting married. She smiled briefly for the first time since I had arrived.

She said, "Tell me more about your parents. What kind of people were they? What kind of family things did you do when you were growing up?"

I said, "My parents lived in a house very much like the one Adam and I now have. My mother could have only one child. She was a good woman and she had hundreds of friends. My parents loved each other and spent every minute with each other. They loved me. We had picnics, went fishing, and hiked in the forest preserves."

"Did you ever tell me how you met your friends Hilda, Gabrielle, and Fiora?"

I thought Barbara had given up asking questions of my past. Now, at this stressful juncture, she wanted to discuss my life before Adam. What should I say? How should I answer her? I really didn't want this conversation today, but to appease her, I went for it.

I agreed to share. "You may remember I told you my parents died in a tragic accident. They were biking when a drunk driving a pickup truck killed them. My dad was a lawyer. Jack was his best friend and law partner. When I thought my life was over, Jack was the one who rescued me and helped me pick up the pieces. I took a year off after high school and traveled to Europe."

I paused to gain strength to continue. "In England, I met Gabrielle and her girlfriend while they were hiking. We became friends. They invited me to stay with them at their place in London. The three of us were dancing in the street outside of a pub, when a terrorist attack occurred. Shrapnel sliced into my body and Gabrielle's girlfriend was killed. Gabrielle rescued me. She saved my life. She brought me to Hilda's clinic to deal with the emotional scars."

Barbara gasped. "I stayed at the clinic for over seven months. Fiora was my room-mate."

Stunned, Barbara seemed genuinely sorry. "I never knew. Adam only told me that you were unable to have a child. As young as you are, you have had to cope with more tragedy than most people would see in a lifetime. I don't know how you survived. On a personal note, you are the daughter I always wanted."

"I survived because of the grace of God and the people who befriended me. I want you to know I have grown to love you, too."

The clock ticked off three hours and the doctor came into the surgical waiting room. He was wearing scrubs. Sweat poured from his brow. He cleared his throat.

"Regretfully, I must tell you that your husband did not make it through surgery. We tried everything we could to save his life, but his heart wasn't strong enough."

Barbara collapsed in my arms.

The next few days were a surreal, miserable blur. The death certificate we received from the hospital read: 'Greg Cohen died at 9.09 a.m.; Tuesday, August 12, 2014, from cancer complications.'

Once again, my world was shattered as I dealt with another death. I called Adam's brother, Seth, who was in Thailand. I gave him the terrible news. He promised to take the next flight, so he could be in Chicago before the Friday burial.

Before leaving the hospital, Barbara signed numerous pages of required forms. I don't think she read any of the words on those forms. I took Barbara back to the hotel and walked with her, hand-in-hand, down the hall. Once she was tucked into bed, I booked our flights back to Chicago. While Barbara was still asleep, I returned to the hospital to coordinate the arrangements for a car to transport Greg's body to the airport.

By the time I got it figured out, Barbara was awake and had ordered room service. I made sure she ate and showered, and put on clean clothes. Together, we called Mindy at Shalom Funeral Home to arrange a Friday afternoon burial.

I attempted to call Adam several times, but he refused to accept my call.

Since he didn't respond, I sent him a text, saying: 'Your dad's internment approx. two p.m., Friday at Shalom. Funeral services are at Beth El starting at noon. You must be there by eleven. Shiva is Saturday night through Friday. Don't disappoint your mom.'

My phone pinged with Adam's response. He wrote: 'Too busy. Funeral must be Sunday. Shiva no more than one day, Sunday only.'

Infuriated, I picked up my phone and called Boeing headquarters. Barbara was disgusted with Adam's text. She waited to see my reaction. She seemed stunned with my response.

In spite of my anger, my voice was as cold as a block of ice. "Bob McRoy, please. Tell him it's Marci Cohen."

After two minutes, Bob picked up. He was a vice president of the North American operations.

I said, "Bob, it's Marci. I apologize for calling you like this, but one of our project managers is suffering from stress, he's irrational and he should be relieved from his current assignment."

Bob asked, "Who is this person?"

"My husband, Adam. His father passed away today, and Adam says he doesn't have time to attend his father's funeral. For the last sixty days, he has been working eighteen-hour days and sleeping in his office. I would appreciate it if you would investigate." We talked for a couple of minutes and he promised to call me back.

I put down my phone. Barbara's eyes and mouth were wide open. She didn't know if she should thank me or be angry for possibly sabotaging Adam's career.

Back in Chicago, Bob took the elevator to Adam's floor and knocked on his office door.

Adam yelled. "Who's there? What do you want now?"

Bob walked into the office with a smile on his face and asked Adam, "How are things going, buddy?"

"Bob, we have a crisis in Asia. Problems with the quality of manufacturing and those foreign factories do not believe in delivering their shipments on time. But I will get them in line."

Bob replied, "I am sorry to hear about your father."

Adam appeared stunned that he knew. "Yes, thank you. The funeral is Sunday. I will not allow his death to interfere with our project. We must get this plane out, on schedule and only I can get the job done right."

Bob thought carefully before responding. "Adam, you know that you are permitted to take time off, especially when there is a death in the family. We have good people who can help you and takeover this project while you take a bereavement leave."

Bob noticed Adam's hands were shaking, and his left eye was twitching.

Adam said, "Thank you, but I am the only one who can manage this crisis." All the phones in his office began to ring simultaneously. "I need to take this call. It's the Chinese factory. We will talk later."

Bob left Adam's office only to return an hour later with a security guard. "Adam, I am ordering you to take time off. Hand me your company phone and building pass. I do not want to see you back here for at least two weeks. You are on a medical furlough until you have received clearance from our medical staff to return to work."

Bewildered, Adam walked out of his office and barely crossed the threshold when he collapsed to the floor. He cried like a baby, vomited, and became disoriented. He had difficulty recognizing his co-workers when they came to his aid.

When my phone rang, I recognized the number.

Bob said, "I appreciate you alerting me to Adam's issues. It must have been a tough call for you to make. Your husband collapsed and is disoriented. An ambulance is taking him to Swedish Covenant's psychiatric unit. Adam's secretary will accompany him to the hospital. Early indications are that he had a nervous breakdown. Are you able to go the hospital to handle the paperwork?"

"Oh my gosh! Bob, I am in Houston with Adam's mother. We will not be returning to Chicago until sometime tomorrow. Can it wait until then?"

Bob said, "My condolences to you and your family. I will take care of the issues regarding his admittance.

Is there anything I can do for you? If you need anything, don't hesitate to call me."

That night, I held Barbara like a child in the hotel room's king-sized bed. She shared with me countless stories and memories from when she first met Greg, when they dated and the early years of marriage. She rambled on for hours. It was her therapy. She did not even think before she shared stories that were personal family secrets. It sounded like she had marital issues at one point and possible infidelity.

The next morning was cloudy. We flew with the casket back to Chicago. Neither of us spoke until the funeral home personnel picked us up at the airport. From there, the hearse took us to the funeral home.

Adam did not attend his father's funeral. He remained in the hospital for another month. Boeing gave Adam a paid three-month leave of absence while he recovered. During that time, Adam participated in intensive therapy sessions. Eventually, he returned as the loving and good man I had married.

Erin delivered us our first child. We decided to name her Georgia. I always liked that name. Barb appreciated that we chose a name to honor Greg's memory. Three years later, Erin took a year off to give birth to our second child. We named her Debra after my mother.

Chapter 34

Adam resumed work at Boeing. After three years he was working full-time and had the confidence of his superiors to assume more responsibilities.

I wanted to continue working but Boeing kept making more demands of me, so I retired. I wanted to spend time with our daughters. However, I did find a cutting-edge, high-tech company in need of my technical skills. The office was not far from the house. I agreed to work twenty hours a week from home or at the office as needed.

The lawsuit that Jack filed years ago settled after two appeals. Money could not replace my parents and, at first, Jack was reluctant, but I insisted he take his normal legal fees.

"Jack, it's only money. Millions of dollars will not bring back my parents. Your monies were well earned and will fund your grandchildren's education all the way through graduate school. Besides, I have enough money to last a lifetime. I don't want your share," I assured him.

We had Jack prepare legal documents to establish a children's trust for Georgia, Debra and any other future children which I funded with some of the proceeds.

Every so often, my mind still returned to the past. I recalled the day on the bridge over the Aira Force Waterfalls in England, when Cristina, Gabrielle and I threw our coins into the waterfalls. I prayed for a good family, a loving partner and children. My wishes came true: I have a husband and two beautiful daughters, whom I love with all my heart. I love Adam, he is an affectionate lover and my best friend.

Barbara visits to play with her grandchildren three days a week. Georgia loves her Grammy. Last Friday night, when Barbara was over for dinner, we lit the Sabbath candles. I glanced down and noticed that Georgia joined us. She put her little hands over her eyes as she said the prayer with us. I wish I could have snapped a picture at that moment.

Barbara posted photographs on her Facebook pages of Georgia and her little sister. Debbie was named after my mother. I hoped that the girls will always remember that their Grammy and their parents love them.

After Houston, my relationship with Barbara changed. She treated me as the daughter she never had. I am sure my mom and Barb would have been the best of friends, had they known each other.

I thought things couldn't have been better, until Adam called me to say, "Great news! Boeing is transferring me to the military aircraft division after I clear the security check."

I tried to sound excited for Adam's benefit as I asked, "What kind of security checks?"

"Essentially, the FBI investigates our birth certificates to verify that we are not Russian spies. It should be a walk in the park, comrade."

I knew he was joking, but his words sent a chill down my spine.

He continued. "They make sure that we were not in the Communist Party when we were in grade school. They want to verify all aspects of our past. Don't worry! No one has ever failed this test and stayed out of jail."

"Very funny. How long does the security process take? Is there anything we should do?"

"Assume the phones and television are bugged. The red raven cries at night."

"You are such a funny man. Go back to work. We'll talk later. Love you."

Little did he know that when he mentioned verification, it scared me to no end! My original birth certificate would reveal facts that may cause him to leave me. I thought that my birth gender would never haunt me again. Yet, it was rearing its ugly head.

Every day, I was on tenterhooks, hoping that Adam was granted his security clearance. I prayed that my name and past would remain my secrets. I couldn't sleep, knowing that I may be exposed. I reflected that if I have the chance to live my life over, knowing what I know and surviving the events of my life, I would still have chosen the same path, time and time again. I love my life. I love my spouse. I love my children. I treasure my friends. This road was my destiny.

Hilda would often remind me. "You are one of the very few individuals to live through what you did and find happiness. You should count your blessings and be thankful."

Those words gave me strength while the FBI performed their security clearance investigation. I was in the kitchen making breakfast for the kids; we were running late. As I rushed around, I kept thinking of the story I read of the escaped con, who was apprehended after thirty-five years on the run.

Today, Adam volunteered to take Georgia to preschool after seeing how stressed out I was. Grammy was in the next room rocking Debra in the chair when the front doorbell rang.

"Shit, I do not have time for this," I said. I had no idea who was at the door. I was hoping to leave. Maybe I could still sneak out through the garage without being seen and make it to the office for my morning meeting. I looked down the driveway and I saw a large sedan parked behind my car. The doorbell rang again.

I yelled, "Coming! I will be there in a moment."

I looked through the peephole and then opened the door to find a nicely dressed woman in ugly shoes, flashing a badge. Bewildered, I asked, "May I help you?"

"My name is Doris Cutler. I am an FBI agent. Your husband is an employee at Boeing, and I have been assigned to complete the paperwork related to his security clearance. I have a few questions for you."

My heart sank down to my toes. I started to say something stupid but managed to gather my wits. With a faux smile and the most inviting voice I could muster, I said, "Please come in."

"Mrs Cohen, anything that we discuss will remain confidential. However, let me warn you, any false statements made to an agent during the interview process is a violation of federal law. You may be prosecuted if you tell me intentionally inaccurate statements. Do you understand your rights, as I have just explained them to you?"

"Yes. Please call me Marci. I prefer that we speak in the den. My mother-in-law is with my daughter in the family room. I'll need to call my office to tell them that I will be late today."

My heart was beating a mile a minute. *This must be how it feels to walk to the gallows*, I thought, as we headed into the den. I was getting sick to my stomach.

"Please sit down."

I offered her a chair and I sat on the couch.

We talked for an hour. She asked me a series of questions from a preprinted checklist. I was honest and truthful, and I began to relax. She confirmed that I had been a victim of a terrorist attack and that my parents were no longer living. The FBI questionnaire didn't ask if one had had gender-related surgery. I didn't know if I should feel relieved or if I should pack my bags and run for the hills. Should I continue to follow Gabrielle's advice, or should I trust my husband and bare my soul by telling the truth after all these years? Paralyzed, I did nothing and followed the agent's lead.

After an hour and a half, she left. Now, all I could do was wait for the FBI report.

Months passed and the FBI was off my radar. I was in the kitchen, preparing breakfast, when I heard Adam call to me from the top of the stairs.

"Bad news! I flunked the security clearance check. They want me to report to the office to discuss it."

Shivers of fear ran down my spine. I was terrified. I wanted to come clean before he heard it from a stranger, but I was too scared to tell him.

As he walked down the stairs toward the kitchen, I thought I heard him singing an up-beat melody. Were my ears playing tricks on me?

"Dear, are you burning the toast?" he said.

Something didn't seem right. He didn't seem angry or depressed. Yes, I was burning the toast and everything else. I could not concentrate on anything but my fear.

I stuttered, "No, nothing is burning. I'm getting Georgia off to preschool. Why aren't you bummed or angry? I thought you really wanted the promotion?"

I threw the toast in the garbage and poured a bowl of cereal for Georgia as I waited for his answer.

"Don't worry, no big deal. Can you arrange for Mom to babysit tonight? Thinking we should go downtown for dinner."

"I don't know. What's up? Are we celebrating you *not* getting the job?"

"Honey, I'm pulling your leg. I just received an email from Bob. I passed and I start the new position on Monday."

I screamed at the top of my lungs. Adam thought I was happy for him. Little did he know how relieved I was for myself.

I shouted, "You shithead! Why did you lie to me? I will call Barbara right away. Should we go to Gibson's?"

He swept me into arms with a tremendous hug just as Georgia walked into the kitchen.

She walked up to us and asked, "Mommy, why is Daddy a shithead?"